keeping her secret

an Endless Summer novel

SARAH NICOLAS

Entangled Publishing, LLC
2614 South Timberline Road
Suite 109
Fort Collins, CO 80525
Visit our website at www.entangledpublishing.com.

Crush is an imprint of Entangled Publishing, LLC.

Edited by Stacy Abrams
Cover design by Heather Howland
Cover art from Shutterstock

Manufactured in the United States of America

First Edition July 2016

For Allison, who has no idea she gave me the strength to accept myself.

Chapter One

Riya's toe caught on the rock embedded in the gravel path, and she lurched before catching herself. Her duffel bag tilted forward, jerking her arm with it until the sturdy canvas smacked against the ground. She glanced around and breathed a sigh of relief. All the campers near enough to see were too absorbed in pre-camp excitement to have noticed.

The sun beat harshly down on her bronze skin. Sweat prickled her neck, so she swept her thick black hair into a lazy ponytail.

Riya hoisted the bag back to her shoulder and walked on, the lake on her right and cabins on her left. Boys milled about these cabins, ages increasing as she walked along. Somehow, the front porches were already draped in towels and half-dried clothes. She'd obviously gone the wrong way from the parking lot. The girls' cabins must be the identical, but tidier, lineup on the other side of the lake.

Her mom's car had overheated, and she'd arrived almost an hour after check-in, too shy to ask anyone for directions. Riya'd seen the error of her ways since then. She told herself she'd stop the next employee she saw. She considered asking one of the boys for about half a second before chickening out.

Gravel crunched under approaching steps. Riya jerked her gaze up to find an overly perky girl wearing a baseball cap with "Camp Pine Ridge" embroidered across it practically bouncing toward her.

"I'm Camp Counselor Becky," the girl said, voice chirping like a bird. "You look a little lost?"

Becky smiled up at her with so much joy it should've been fake. But it wasn't. Riya had always been suspicious of people who seemed so happy they were about to burst out of their skin with it. Not natural.

Becky was only a couple years older than Riya and ridiculously cute with huge hazel eyes and a freckled button nose. She'd certainly have no shortage of campers harboring secret crushes over the next couple of weeks. If it weren't for the supernatural levels of cheer, Riya would probably be one of them.

Riya smiled back at Becky with a mere fraction of her happiness. "Do you know where cabin G7A is?"

Becky nodded so enthusiastically Riya worried for the muscular health of her neck. She pointed farther down the path. "I'm actually the counselor assigned to your cabin. You must be Riya. I was just headed to the parking lot to meet you."

She paused and peered up at Riya expectantly. Riya knew her five-six height was considered perfectly average, but she always thought of herself as short. Probably because she spent all her time around volleyball players. Becky bounced, drawing Riya's attention to the fact that she was waiting for Riya's response.

"Great?" Riya hadn't intended for it to come out as a question. "So it's…" she trailed off, searching the other side of the lake as if she might see the cabin number from there.

"You went the wrong way, I'm afraid. But go ahead and walk past the arts and crafts hut—you can't miss it; it's the one with the huge windows—and yours will be the second cabin."

Riya took a few steps backward, maintaining eye contact with Becky as she said, "Thank you." Then, she spun on her heel and picked up the pace toward the cabin.

Sweat trickled down Riya's neck as she approached the arts and crafts building. As Becky promised, windows made up two entire sides of the building. Between blinding flashes of reflected sunlight, a flicker of movement inside the room caught Riya's attention.

She veered closer, stepping off of the gravel path onto the patchy grass. The bursts of movement coalesced into a ballet dancer, twirling and leaping with singular grace. A blond bun swirled high upon her head. Black tights and a pale blue fitted tank stretched across her tall, lean frame. In the seconds when the movement slowed and the glare on the glass moved in just the right way, Riya thought the girl looked familiar. Of their own accord, her feet led her toward the propped-open door. She entered, thinking of nothing else besides getting a better view of the supremely talented dancer.

Music played from a portable speaker the size of a soda can in one corner. The dancer slid and spun and flew across a worn wooden floor. She moved with so much passion, so much soul, that Riya stood riveted two steps inside the doorway, sure her mouth hung open in admiration but unable to bring herself to care how it looked. This—the dancer and the dance, combined, inseparable—was the most beautiful thing she'd ever seen.

Glimpses of the ballerina's face crashed against her memories, leaving her on the teetering edge of recognition.

Then, another person she hadn't noticed before moved in the corner and several things happened at once. The second person was a guy she also recognized, which made everything fall into place. The dancer stumbled to a stop, staring at Riya, drawing the guy's attention to her as well. Riya's duffel bag thudded to the floor.

"Riya?" the guy said, voice hopeful, happy, excited.

"Riya!" the girl said, voice none of those things. The very opposite of those things.

The two were twins. Colt Chastain was the masculine version of his willowy sister, Courtney—all blue eyes and blond hair and winking dimples and skin like velvety whipped cream.

And up until four years ago, they had been Riya's best friends.

All the air sucked out of the room when Riya's gaze discovered the agitation roiling out of Courtney's every pore. She was twelve again, heart shattered and stomped to bits in the backyard she'd be leaving in three days.

Colt bounded to Riya and swept her into a celebratory hug. "Riya!" he said. "I thought I'd never see you again."

He pulled back and grinned at her, a grin Riya tried to return and failed miserably, resulting in something that felt like a grimace. Colt was kind enough to pretend not to notice.

"You never called or emailed. We worried." Colt glanced back at his sister but then turned quickly away from her death glare. He squeezed Riya's shoulders. "I missed you."

Riya regained enough composure to mumble, "Missed you, too, Colt." She swallowed down a lump the size of Texas, before mustering the bravery to look at Courtney again. Despite her obvious resentment, the girl glowed in the golden light of sunset, as beautiful as she'd ever been. Dancing had served her well, packing her lithe frame with lean muscle and matchless grace.

"Missed you too, Courtney."

The spell broke as Courtney's scowl deepened.

"Oh, hell no." Courtney stomped past the two of them,

her shoulder brushing Riya's as she passed.

The beautiful ballerina disappeared into the blinding light just as Riya did something she hadn't done in four years: burst into tears.

. . .

Courtney's feet pounded the gravel all the way back to her bunk as she ignored excited waves and several calls of "Hey, Court!" from campers she'd spent the last couple of summers hanging out with. She could count on one hand the number of boys her age here who she *hadn't* kissed—and the ones who didn't want to kiss her? Well, she didn't need any digits for that.

Didn't Riya Johnson know this was Courtney's summer camp? Who did she think she was, strolling into Camp Pine Ridge in their last year with her big, sad brown eyes, like she had any right?

This was Courtney's last summer, her final fling before she had to commit to her family's vision for the rest of her life. And she was not about to let Riya ruin it for her.

She'd spent four years trying to forget that crisp autumn night right before Riya moved.

She had only been moving one county over, but to thirteen-year-old Courtney, it felt a million miles away. They'd been climbing a huge oak tree in Riya's backyard. Well, Riya had already climbed up to the top and back down to encourage Courtney to go even higher. Riya had always been the brave one.

She'd lowered herself to the same branch Courtney straddled, then scooted until she sat mere inches away. "I'm going to miss you, Courtney," she'd said, threading her short, strong fingers through Courtney's pale, slender ones, as she'd done a dozen times.

Courtney remembered being fascinated by Riya's lips, fading from a deep brown on the edges to a pale pink in the plump center. She stared at them until she licked her own lips and closed her eyes without thinking. The next thing she knew, those beautiful lips were pressed against hers and Riya was kissing her like she'd seen in movies and Courtney was kissing her back. Riya's arms had circled Courtney's waist, and Courtney's fingers traced circles on the back of Riya's neck. She hadn't been thinking about what any of it meant. She'd just been reacting and doing what felt right.

Then the porch door slammed, and they jumped apart. Colt called their names, and Courtney scrambled away from Riya, shimmying down the tree trunk and running all the way home.

She'd never talked to Riya again.

Courtney had kissed dozens of boys in the past four years, but none of them had felt as right and as wonderful as Riya's clumsy lips pressed against hers on that chilly September night.

And that was the whole problem.

A small someone stood in her path. The kid didn't move as she stomped forward. Courtney glanced up to see a skinny first-year redheaded girl staring at her own feet.

"Fozzie Bear sent me to get you," she said without looking up. "Your mom's on the phone. She's called six times."

Inhaling, Courtney straightened her shoulders and raised her head. "Thanks, kid."

As Courtney made her way toward the office, the girl followed several feet back and continued to avoid looking at her. All around them, the lush mountain summer offered every hue of green imaginable. The afternoon sun hung low in the sky, leaving a long trail of fire across the lake.

Courtney slowed her pace to walk next to the girl. "What's your name?"

The girl bit her lip, displaying a wide gap between her two front teeth, as she watched her feet take several steps. "Olivia."

"Are you scared of me, Olivia?"

Nodding, Olivia scrunched her eyes, wrinkling her freckled nose. The poor kid was terrified.

Courtney pivoted and bent at the waist in front of Olivia, stopping her in her tracks. "Why?"

The girl took two steps back. "The other girls in G1A said you were mean. One said you duct tape girls to trees."

Courtney laughed, but when Olivia's green eyes went wide, she stifled it quickly. "That was just the one time, and she deserved it, I promise."

Finally, Olivia glanced up at her through strawberry-blond lashes. "So you're not mean?"

"No." Courtney slowly reached out to straighten the girl's shirt. "That's just something people say about girls when they don't let other people push them around."

Olivia met Courtney's gaze straight on. "Nobody pushes you around?"

"No, nobody." *Except my parents.*

Olivia's eyes began to change shape, and the transition spread across her entire face until she smiled brightly. "Then I'm going to be mean, too." She took off in the opposite direction from the office, practically skipping.

"That's not what I meant!" Courtney called after her, but the girl was gone, probably off to cause untold trouble. Laughing to herself, Courtney shook her head and continued on to the office. She made a mental note to have a better talk with the girl later.

Camp director Bob Fazio—or Fozzie Bear, as he was known among the campers—was not in the office, but his secretary wordlessly motioned to a phone in the corner with a flashing red light. She offered Courtney a sympathetic smile.

"I tried to tell her campers aren't allowed to use the phone for personal calls," she said. "But, well, you know."

Oh good Lord did Courtney know.

Courtney cradled the phone between her ear and her shoulder. "Hey, Mom." She raised her left foot behind her and pulled it against her thigh for a quad stretch. Riya had cut her dance practice short, but she still had a couple of things to work through before camp events started, and she needed to stay limber.

"Hay is for horses, Courtney."

Courtney's eyes rolled back of their own accord. Seriously, she couldn't help it. "Hello, Mother."

"Was the new driver okay?" Unmistakable traffic sounds filled the background of her mother's call. Courtney pictured her, black heels clicking briskly through the downtown streets of Charlotte in her crisp business suit, hair unmoving from half a can of hair spray.

"Yes, he was fine." Her brother had chatted him up throughout the entire three-hour drive, but her mother wouldn't care to know that.

"Just fine?" Mrs. Chastain's voice went shrill. "I don't know why your father insisted on hiring a Mexican anyway."

Blood rushed to Courtney's cheeks, embarrassed even though no one else could hear. "He was great," she amended. "Perfect gentleman. And his parents are from Argentina."

"Anyway," her mother said, already bored with the conversation. "I spoke to Joseph Morgan about getting you an internship next summer, and he said it wouldn't be a problem."

Courtney had lowered her left leg and started to raise her right, but stopped in mid-motion. Her mother had called her on the first day of summer camp to talk about an internship next summer. It was like she was *trying* to ruin Courtney's final few months of freedom.

"An internship? Isn't next summer too early?" Her heart thudded clumsily against her chest. It seemed to be saying: *Too soon. Too soon.*

"You'll need to start early in order to be up to working for Chastain and Chastain when you graduate law school. You'll start with menial tasks. Filing, getting coffee, that kind of thing. You can do it."

Courtney had no doubt that she could do it, but no one had ever asked her if she actually *wanted* to. She sighed, wondering if it was even worth it to bring up that old argument. She never won. With the two best defense attorneys in the old south as parents, she hadn't won a single argument since she was four years old.

Oh, what the hell. She'd told Olivia she didn't let anyone push her around. Besides, her mother was hundreds of miles and four weeks away. "And what if I get in to Juilliard?"

Her mother huffed. "Courtney Clare Chastain, I thought we agreed. Your dancing is a lovely hobby that will keep you slim and graceful as you age. But it's not a *career*."

Only Collette Chastain would consider her unilateral decree a mutual agreement. And call something Courtney practiced sixteen hours a week "a hobby."

"But that's the whole point of Juilliard," Courtney argued for the billionth time. "People who graduate from there *can* make it a career."

"Your father and I won't pay for it." Her mother's voice came out clipped and angry. She'd never spelled it out in so many words, usually choosing to rely on veiled threats instead. But there it was in black and white. It seemed Courtney wasn't the only one emboldened by the distance between them.

Most parents would be thrilled if their daughter managed to snag one of the twelve spots offered each year to women in Juilliard's dance program. Not hers, though. She'd known since she'd understood the basic concept of jobs: the only acceptable path included Harvard Law and a fast track to partnership at Chastain and Chastain.

"I don't need you to." Courtney's voice had fallen flat, attempting to conceal her fear with icy determination.

She was lying, of course. All of Juilliard's scholarships were need-based, and her family certainly didn't qualify in that department. If she even managed to get in.

"Courtney, you can't pay tuition with a pretty smile." Her mother's syrupy sweet words grated against her nerves like sandpaper.

The worst part was, Courtney couldn't argue with her. She didn't see how she'd make it four years without her parents' support. And they'd never give it. This conversation would never end any differently.

"Okay, Mother, I have to go. We have orientation." *In forty minutes,* she added silently. But after this wonderful conversation, Courtney needed some dance time.

"Kisses," her mother said.

Courtney placed the receiver back on its base. When she walked out the door, she realized she hadn't mentioned seeing Riya. But why would she? Her mother had never been rude to her friend, but she'd let slip little comments in the years after Riya moved away in her patented passive-aggressive style. *Maybe now you can make some* quality *friends*, she'd said. And *Isn't Junior Cotillion so much better than playing in the dirt with that girl?*

No, there was no reason to mention it to her mother. Not that it mattered, anyway. Riya's presence meant nothing. As Courtney stepped from the shadow of the building into the bright sunlight, she declared she'd treat Riya as exactly that: nothing. As far as Courtney was concerned, Riya Johnson did not exist.

Chapter Two

"I'll see you at the welcome thing?" Colt asked Riya as they reached the steps leading up to Cabin G7A.

He'd walked her the rest of the way, promising her Courtney's reaction earlier had nothing to do with her. She'd been having a rough day, he'd said, courtesy of their mother. That made sense, at least. Mrs. Chastain had always been a real ball-buster, even when they were kids. But Riya wasn't convinced. The way those blue eyes had stared at her—like she were the last person on Earth Courtney'd ever hoped to see again—left her stomach tied into tiny knots.

"Yeah." Riya tried to infuse the word with cheer and hope but, judging by Colt's sympathetic half-smile, she'd failed.

The setting sun glinted off his golden hair as he slowly backed away. "Come over as soon as you can. I'll introduce you to the guys."

"Thank you, Colt," she said, meaning it with every cell in her body.

Riya swung open the door and quickly discovered all the beds but one had been claimed, so she tossed her bag on a top bunk in the back corner. Her bunkmate was nowhere to be seen, but a classic brown and gold Louis Vuitton rolling suitcase asserted ownership over the lower bed. What kind of teenager brought a bag like that to a summer camp in the woods?

All around her, girls unpacked their things into the small dressers provided at the foot of each bed in between casting shy glances at one another. Every now and then, a pair would squeal and hug and talk about how happy they were to see each other again. They slowly filtered out in pairs and trios. Riya shrugged, deciding to abandon her half-unpacked duffel in favor of exploring the camp. She'd unpack later that night. Or tomorrow. Eventually.

She itched to check out the facilities. Her parents had picked this place based on a brochure, of all things, so she had no idea what to expect. The pamphlet had said they had volleyball, but that was no guarantee. Some places strung a droopy rope crookedly over an uneven, sandy rock pit and called it volleyball. And who knew if enough decent players even came to this camp to give her a good workout?

Riya wasn't about to let a lazy summer put her off her game after nabbing an impossible St. John's Academy scholarship and verbal promises of college offers if she played a stellar senior season. Her parents couldn't afford the St. John's tuition, so if she lost that scholarship, she'd have to transfer to another school in the middle of her senior year. Bye-bye college ball and so long "world-class academics."

"I wouldn't take that bed if it were the last one on Earth," a voice said from behind her.

Riya turned and found a sturdy Latina peering at her. Slanted afternoon sunlight filtered in through the windows, casting stark shadows on her face and thick, shoulder-length wavy hair.

"Might as well be," she said. "It's the last open spot in the cabin. I guess I got in a little late."

The other girl shrugged. "Still." She strode toward Riya with a confidence in movement reserved for competitive athletes. "The queen bee doesn't much like us jocks."

"Us?" Riya raised an eyebrow. With her casual style and lean muscle, she wasn't usually assumed to be a jock on first glance.

The girl motioned to Riya's duffel, with her number written on it. "What do you play?"

Riya felt a smile tug at the corners of her lips. "Volleyball, mostly. Some soccer, but not on the same level. You?"

"Softball's my moneymaker, but I ride the varsity bench for basketball. I've played volleyball on the beach with friends." She said the last part as though it was an apology.

Riya laughed. "Well, I've never touched a softball, so... I'm Riya."

"Dee," she said with a nod. "We play a lot of everything around here, so you'll have the chance to learn softball."

"Perfect." Riya found herself unable to hold back the grin spreading across her face. A couple of minutes in and she'd already found her people. Or, rather, they'd found her. It was a good thing Dee had spoken first. If it were up to Riya, she'd scrounge up the courage to introduce herself right about the time they all went home.

"And thanks for the heads up on my bunkmate," she added, "but I don't have much of a choice."

Dee grimaced, then offered a sympathetic smile. "It should make things interesting, at least. The jocks and the royals have had an ongoing prank war since before I started coming here three years ago." She returned to her bunk across the room and rifled through her own duffel bag.

Royals. Queen bee. Riya smirked at the Louis Vuitton bag on her bunk. She knew the type, all right. "Have I just been drafted into that war?" She'd gone to volleyball camp for the past several years and was no stranger to a friendly exchange of shenanigans.

"Either that or you're collateral damage." Dee pulled out an elastic and tamed her voluminous waves into something halfway between a bun and a ponytail. She then pulled out a roll of craft twine and a sleeve of pink princess party cups, holding them up with a dangerous smirk. "Care to fire the first shot of the summer?"

Instinctively, Riya scanned the bunkhouse. They were alone, the other girls having all gone out onto the porch together. A twinge of unease tickled the back of her neck. Pranking someone she hadn't even met seemed mean. But Dee did say it was ongoing, so it wouldn't be unexpected.

Dee didn't miss her hesitation. "No biggie if you're not ready. But it's going to happen either way. And you'll definitely get hit at some point, so might as well strike early."

Riya cast one more glance at the cabin door before shrugging. "It's all in good fun, right?"

Grinning at her, Dee said, "Right."

. . .

As soon as she opened the door of her cabin, Courtney spotted the web of string crazily woven over her bed, stretching from all four posts and connecting to the springs supporting the top bed.

Looks like the war has begun.

It was an old camp prank, but a good one. A couple of steps closer, she realized the pranker had upgraded the standard stunt. Her bags and clothes lay in the middle of the mattress near the wall so that she couldn't reach them and pull out her cuticle scissors, like she'd been planning to. Suspended all over the web hung little paper princess party cups filled nearly to the brim with water. If she rushed, she'd dump water all over her stuff. If she waited too long to take it down, the water would soak through the cheap cups and soak her stuff. And the pretty pink dresses and sparkling tiaras printed on the cups were a nice little dig.

"Well played," she muttered to herself as her face flushed with irritation. While she could admire the execution of the prank, she wondered who thought it was okay to start the prank war by making the first move against *her*.

She gently began untying the knots securing the twine to the bedpost. Her mind ran through the list of girls she'd seen earlier that day. That girl Delores could always be counted on for well-executed pranks. Could be her. Whoever it was, she'd make them pay for it.

Riya must have been assigned to G7B, the other cabin for girls their age, since she hadn't turned up during the designated arrival time. Good. Courtney wouldn't have to see her every morning as soon as she woke and every night before falling asleep. Though, as that mental image formed, a thrill shot through her veins, setting her limbs tingling. Courtney clenched her jaw and refocused on freeing her bed from its twine prison. Riya Johnson wouldn't distract Courtney from anything this summer. The next four weeks were hers and hers alone.

The plonk of fat water drops hitting fabric broke her from her thoughts. "Damn it!" One of the cups spilled half of its volume onto the blankets at the foot of the bed before she caught it.

Managing to extricate the maze without spilling any more water, Courtney dropped the twine to the floor so she could yank a change of clothes and her makeup bag from her suitcase. After changing into her flirtiest outfit of a flowy powder-pink tank top and hip-hugging white shorts, Courtney went to the mirror to reapply her makeup—her armor, as her mother had called it. The welcome talk began in just a few minutes.

She would wait until almost everyone gathered in the cafeteria, making a strategic, dramatic entrance. All eyes on Courtney, as usual.

Including Riya's, she realized, before wiping away that thought with a swipe of her favorite lip gloss.

But when she tried to sweep eyeliner across her lid, her hand shook too hard to draw a straight line. She surrendered, tossing the pencil into the bag, and settled for brushing a light pink powder across her cheeks and on her eyelids to contrast her baby blues.

Courtney shook her head and turned slowly away from her own reflection.

When dropping her makeup at her bunk, she noticed someone had claimed the bunk on top of hers with a dirty duffel bag displaying the number 4 drawn in black permanent marker. Someone who didn't know better than to share a sleeping structure with Courtney Chastain. And a jock, by the look of it. Talk about adding insult to injury.

Swift payback would be just the thing to get her mind off of her unfortunate blast from the past. Riya's presence changed nothing, she told herself. The game plan was still the same: chill on the lake, flirt with all the boys, kiss half the boys, and ignore how none of it made her feel a damn thing.

When she lugged the duffel over the edge of the bed, it dropped to the floor with a dull thud. Something small and brown rolled across the floor, spinning in on its own path, circling the wooden floor until it tottered and fell onto its side. It was a roll of twine. An exact match to the stuff she'd just untied from her bed.

A wicked smile inched across Courtney's shiny pink lips as she leaned over and picked up the twine. She'd have to be a couple of minutes late to the welcome event. Poetic vengeance would be just the thing to get her back on track.

Chapter Three

Riya sat on her hands, trying to pretend all of her attention was focused anywhere besides the cafeteria doorway. They'd eaten the traditional first-night spaghetti dinner, and the counselors had started introducing themselves and other camp staff two minutes ago, yet Courtney still wasn't there. Could she be so upset by Riya's presence that she wouldn't show up?

Riya usually found comfort in the standardization of cafeterias across the nation. Whether it was a barely funded public school, a swanky private academy like St. John's, a hospital, or — apparently — a summer camp, all cafeterias had basically the same look and equipment. And with as many times as Riya had changed schools, that sort of familiarity could be soothing.

Colt hadn't let her dwell on Courtney's reaction earlier, introducing her to his friends and practically drowning her in questions. If only Courtney could be as happy to catch up as her twin had been. They *had* been best friends once.

A parade of people streamed in front of the room, Riya

managing to catch the barest details. Bob Fazio, the director, stood not much taller than the eleven-year-olds and seemed like the kind of guy several kids called Uncle Bobby. Betsy, the cook, gave a single wave and the flash of a smile before returning to the kitchen.

Then came Dane and Dewey, the lifeguards. No relation, despite the alliteration. One was an Australian Abercrombie model-in-training, making the girls in the room sit up straighter, and the other was scrawny and obviously nervous in front of such a crowd, which Riya could certainly relate to. She couldn't remember which was which.

Then came Jacob, who elicited whispers from the girls around Riya when Bob introduced him as his nephew and junior counselor. Nancy, a kind-looking woman, was introduced as the arts and crafts director.

A breeze ruffled her ponytail, and Riya's gaze snapped to the door. Courtney strolled in like a freaking Nordic goddess with her head held high, cheeks flushed and skin glowing. Sun-kissed legs stretched up from a pair of sparkly sandals for miles and miles until finally disappearing under the hem of low-hung white shorts. Flashes of smooth stomach teased as her pink top moved with every graceful step.

Riya's heart pounded in her chest. Courtney Chastain was trying to kill her. That outfit was a perfectly crafted murder weapon. Checking to make sure her mouth didn't hang open, Riya tore her gaze from Courtney and swallowed. Hard.

Beside her, Colt slid down the bench, away from Riya. Riya didn't know why until Courtney froze five feet from them. She glanced at Riya then shook her head at her brother. Colt rolled his eyes in response, patting the sliver of bench between them.

"Miss Chastain, please take your seat so we may continue," Bob Fazio called, a small chuckle breaking through his voice.

It was then Riya noticed she wasn't the only one distracted

by Courtney's entrance. Excluding her brother, every boy in the room age twelve to eighteen stared in their direction—and some of the girls, too.

Riya watched a wide range of emotions pass over Courtney's face in less than a second before she straightened her shoulders in some kind of resolve. Her hair tumbled to her elbows in gentle waves. Sighing, she tossed the golden strands over her shoulder before spinning and squeezing her hips between Riya and Colt.

The welcome talk continued, but Riya only caught fleeting fragments of the briefing. Something about the daily schedule and a talent show on the last day. Approximately 98 percent of her attention narrowed in on the seven inches of Courtney's white-silk skin pressed against Riya's outer thigh.

Riya took a deep breath to steady herself but caught the sweet rose petal scent wafting from Courtney. She inhaled one deep breath, reveling in the heavenly smell, before shaking her head.

Ridiculous. She was being completely ridiculous.

She'd never let anyone have such an overwhelming effect on her. Certainly not someone like Courtney, someone who couldn't—or wouldn't—return her affections. Someone who had broken her heart four years ago and never once looked back.

Riya stared at her own shoelaces, actively un-focusing on the girl sitting next to her.

Trying to, anyway.

Next thing she knew, everyone stood around her and the room buzzed with conversation. The welcome event was over.

"Earth to Riya."

Someone bumped her shoulder with theirs, and she looked up to find Colt's friend Trey smirking at her. Colt had introduced them before they'd sat down, and they'd traded the typical get-to-know-you questions. *Where are you from?*

What do you like to do? That sort of thing.

He had a fun smile, made even more playful by the shaggy mess of chestnut curls flopping around with his every movement. The kind of smile that always received an answer.

"Easy to space out during these things, huh?" he said.

She loosed an embarrassed laugh, grateful for the excuse. "Yeah, I guess so."

He nodded, his smirk spreading into a full-on grin. "You going to the welcome bonfire?"

"Bonfire?" She scanned the room, discovering kids filtering out in small groups. She hadn't heard anything about a bonfire.

"Of course she is," Colt interjected, dropping an arm lazily over Riya's shoulders. "We have four years to catch up on, after all."

Riya felt several people's attention shift to her, both overtly and subtly. Colt Chastain stood out in a crowd. And so did, apparently, anyone he deemed worthy. She squirmed.

"You really knew the twins when they were kids?" Trey asked, wonder in his eyes. "What were they like?"

Riya laughed, remembering. "Colt was pretty much the same." She cast a sideways glance at him, craning her neck to look up. "Except shorter."

Colt laughed.

Trey shrugged as though he expected as much. "And Courtney?"

Courtney turned at the sound of her name, her eyes taking in the situation with mild disapproval.

Riya felt the smile drop from her face. She kept trying to picture Courtney from before, but the only image she could conjure was the moment before she jumped down from that tree and ran away from Riya's kiss. A beat of silence hung awkwardly in the air. Even Trey's easy smile lost some of its repose.

Courtney, of all people, saved her. "Seriously, Trey," she said with a click of her tongue. "You know I've always been perfectly fabulous."

"Aww, come on," he laughed. "I want to hear about Courtney Chastain's awkward years. Before she broke an average of two guys' hearts per day."

Courtney? A man-eater?

"No such thing," Courtney said, placing a hand on her hip.

Colt caught Riya's eye, a smile teasing his lips. Riya tried—and failed—to stifle a laugh.

"You two have something to say?" Courtney asked, threatening in a playful way.

Riya shook her head, laughing. "Nope." She held her hands up in surrender.

"As the legend goes," Colt said, "Courtney came out of the womb so perfect that the doctor instantly retired, claiming he'd never top such a career-defining moment."

A guffaw burst from Riya's mouth. "Awkward, since they had to find another doctor to deliver Colt."

"And so began my life of playing second fiddle to the legendary Courtney Chastain," Colt said.

Courtney laughed while glaring at her brother's sarcasm, and for a fraction of a second, everything felt right. Riya was laughing with her two best friends and the world rotated perfectly on its axis.

"We should get going or all the good logs will be taken." Trey waggled his eyebrows and made for the door.

Only then did Riya realize that everyone else had cleared out of the cafeteria.

Colt and Riya followed him. The three noticed Courtney's absence when they reached the door of the cafeteria and turned to see her standing in the same spot.

Colt's brow wrinkled in confusion. "You coming, Court?"

"Um." She paused. "I'll catch up."

Courtney hadn't changed as much as she wanted everyone to think she had. The girl was still a terrible liar. Maybe it was the laughter they'd shared, or maybe it was glimpsing a crack of vulnerability in Courtney's shell, but a surge of courage rushed through Riya.

Regardless of the way her heart raced at every glimpse of Courtney, and the way her stomach clenched when she remembered the last time they'd parted, she wanted peace.

"Go on." Riya shooed the boys outside. "I need to talk to her, anyway."

Oblivious, Trey threw up his hands. "Girl talk, I see. Can't get in the way of that."

Colt, of course, knew a little bit more. Though, exactly how much, Riya had no idea.

Concern darkened his features. "You sure?" he whispered.

"Yeah, we're here for the next four weeks. We've got to make it work."

He glanced over her shoulder toward his sister and gave Riya a doubtful shrug. "Good luck." He turned, and the two boys shuffled toward the tennis courts.

Courtney startled when Riya returned to the dining hall. She cast panicked glances at the door.

"Everyone's gone," Riya said.

Their aloneness did nothing to calm Courtney. She hugged her arms to her chest and tried to walk past Riya to the door. "I'm just going to find my friend Bridget," she said. "You should catch up with Colt."

"I wanted to talk to you first." Riya didn't block Courtney's way, but she didn't move out of it, either.

"We don't have anything to talk about," Courtney said, but she didn't leave, which encouraged Riya.

"Court," Riya sighed. "We were friends, remember? Not just friends, but best friends. We did everything together."

"I remember." Courtney tightened her arms, squeezing

her stomach. "But you want to be something other than friends."

"No, I don't," Riya said. Both Riya and Courtney had changed in the last four years. Of course, Courtney's beauty had only increased, but that wasn't all there was to it. Riya had no idea whether or not this cold version of Courtney was someone she could forgive for what happened four years ago. "We were kids. It was a stupid kiss. I was experimenting."

"But you do...like girls?" Courtney asked.

Riya ran a hand through her ponytail. "Yeah, I do. I don't hide it anymore." She watched Courtney carefully. "And you don't. Like them, not in that way."

Courtney nodded. "But you don't like me? In that way?"

Trying to read Courtney's expression, Riya took a deep breath. The truth—"I don't know yet. Give me a few days or weeks"—wasn't what Courtney needed to hear. For now, she needed to feel safe. So Riya lied. "You're not really my type, Court."

Courtney's head snapped to attention, and her blue eyes bore down on Riya's face. She'd probably never heard those words aimed at her before. "What *is* your type, then?"

Riya didn't answer right away. Truth was, she didn't know how to answer. As far as she knew, she didn't have a type. She liked individual people, not everyone who checked off criteria on an arbitrary list.

Courtney filled the silence. "That girl Delores plays softball, and she's about as opposite from me as you can get, so—" She stopped speaking at Riya's laugh. "What's so funny?"

"Dee is straight as an arrow." She paused, considering. "And are you trying to set me up?"

Courtney's brow creased in confusion. "But, softball and..." she trailed off.

"You thought she was a lesbian because she plays

softball? You're the last person who should rely so much on stereotypes."

"But she wears black tennis shoes," Courtney insisted.

Riya shrugged. "We weren't all born with your incredible fashion sense."

Courtney's arms dropped to her side as the revelation sunk in. "How do you even know? This is your first day."

"We met. She's in my cabin."

Courtney dropped her gaze and chewed on her lip.

Weird that a simple statement would elicit such a response. "What is it?"

"Delores is in my cabin."

Riya smiled her friendliest smile, despite her stomach plunging. "So that means we're roomies, just like we always talked about." *Great*, Riya thought. That meant she'd have to keep this friendly feelings charade up 24-7.

Silent seconds stretched out between them. Riya steeled herself for her final plea. "Look, this has been so uncomfortable so far. I just want to have fun this summer. I'm sure you do, too. And I'd like for us to be friends again."

Disgust distorted Courtney's features, transforming Riya's stomach into a rock. "I don't want to be friends with you," she said.

Courtney's words nearly knocked her off her feet. It was probably for the best, she told herself. Too many feelings to hide, too many thoughts to keep to herself, otherwise. But still. Courtney was so eager to trash the second chance they'd been given at what had been a truly great friendship. Did she hate her that much?

"Okay," Riya amended, twisting the fingers of her hands together. "Can we have a truce, at least?"

"A truce?" Courtney raised an eyebrow. Not the warm welcome Riya'd been hoping for, but she supposed it could be worse.

"Yeah. I won't try to kiss you again." Riya laughed so Courtney knew she was joking, but it sounded flat to her own ears. "And you can just ignore me." *Like you do everyone else you don't care about.*

Courtney cocked her head to the side, thinking. "Okay." She nodded. "Truce, then."

Riya fought the flashbacks as Courtney dashed away from her once again. She wondered if she'd been cursed to a lifetime of watching her first crush run away.

• • •

Courtney had detoured to her cabin to grab a sweater she didn't really need before joining the bonfire. When she arrived, Riya stood in a circle with Colt, Trey, Delores, a pair of towering twin girls, Courtney's best friend at camp Bridget, and more—including both jocks and her usual crowd. Odd mixture.

She inhaled the cool night air and slowly released the breath before approaching the group. Riya had said to ignore her. Like that was at all possible. Never mind the fact that Riya was totally un-ignorable, but Colt had fully resolved himself to resurrecting their friendship.

Someone had hooked their phone up to a speaker and music joined the sounds of laughing and talking. Cell service didn't venture out here in the mountains, so phones at camp mainly served as jukeboxes and flashlights—and as an alarm, in Courtney's case. Across the field, Trey began shaking his shoulders off the beat, and Riya laughed, joining him in his goofy dance for a few seconds before she blushed and diverted her gaze.

Riya caught sight of Courtney before anyone else noticed and silently watched her make her way through the crowd. Bugs flitted in and out of the smoky air.

Colt's friend David, a huge football-player type with brown hair and brown eyes, offered Courtney a water bottle full of something that looked very much like vodka with a splash of juice. She shook her head. As a rule, she didn't drink. Too many calories and fuzzy mornings made it not conducive to ballet excellence.

"Hey, Courtney," Riya said, meeting her gaze from underneath a veil of thick, dark lashes.

A thrill shot through Courtney's stomach at Riya's quiet confidence and, in that instant, she kinda hated her for it. How dare she make her feel that way after all this time and in front of all her friends? Nobody else had that effect on her. It wasn't fair that Riya, who'd told her she had no feelings for her minutes ago, could.

She'd said Courtney wasn't her type. Whatever that meant.

Courtney clenched her jaw. She had to regain control, to reclaim her status. She smiled, saccharine sweet, at Riya.

"Are you signing up for the talent competition?" she asked. "I remember how lovely you sang when we were kids." Courtney also remembered how shy Riya was about singing in front of people, how she and Colt would have to beg her to sing for them in the privacy of her own living room. No way she'd sing in front of everyone.

Riya's gaze fell to the ground for a second, before rising to meet Courtney's. "You remember that?" she whispered.

Courtney shrugged like it meant nothing. Like she hadn't heard Riya singing in her head as she drifted off to sleep for months after Riya'd moved away.

A soft mauve blushed Riya's cheeks and the tips of her ears. Courtney couldn't help but watch it spread across her skin. Riya shook her head slightly. "I need to focus on staying in shape for volleyball this summer."

Colt bumped Riya's shoulder with his elbow. "Come on,

Ree. You'd be great. Might even give Courtney a run for her perma-title."

Riya raised her eyebrow at him, so he explained. "She's won every year since we started coming here."

"*We've* won," Courtney corrected. "Colt plays piano while I dance. I can't win without him." She felt an unfamiliar need to divert attention away from herself. Riya's eyes focused on her too much, too often.

"They have a piano here?" Riya scanned the bonfire clearing as if she'd find evidence of one.

Colt nodded. "For the music classes. It was covered by a tarp in the cafeteria, in the corner. But I also brought a keyboard, for extra practice."

"Nice."

"I could play for you, too." He turned the full force of his considerable charm on Riya. Most girls agreed to do anything under his gaze. "Do a little Demi Lovato or Ellie Goulding?"

"I'd like to see that!" Trey said.

It was then that Courtney noticed how close their friend stood to Riya, smirking and staring at her for an unnecessarily long time. He brushed her arm or shoulder at every possible moment. Trey couldn't take his eyes off of her.

As if he had any chance with her, even if she didn't like girls.

Trey was okay looking and funny, but Riya was beautiful in such a rare kind of way. She'd inherited her mother's thick, dark hair and incredible bone structure and her father's quiet strength. Her lush lips demanded attention. White men like Courtney's father would call her "exotic," a word Colt said was meant to be complimentary and dehumanizing at the same time. But it was somewhat true. Riya's kind of beauty was captivating and untouchable.

Riya chewed her lip, considering Colt's suggestion. Before she could answer, Colt's eyes lit up with the look that always accompanied his "genius" ideas. An uncomfortable feeling crawled into Courtney's stomach. Her little power play was about to backfire.

"We could do it together, all three of us." His gaze switched excitedly back and forth between Riya and Courtney. "I'll play, Riya sings, Courtney dances. We'd be unstoppable."

Courtney's heart pounded. That would mean spending countless hours over the next four weeks alone with Riya and Colt. Unacceptable. "You and I are already unstoppable," Courtney mumbled.

Riya's advancing smile retreated. "Oh, I wouldn't want to intrude on your tradition. Or ruin your chances."

The tension in Courtney's shoulders softened.

"I'm with Riya," Trey said, nudging her arm with his own. Again. "She should do her own performance. If she's as good as y'all say she is, she might just dethrone the queen."

"That's not—" Riya began, but Colt interrupted her.

"It's settled, then." He grinned at both of them. "Just like the old days when we put on shows for our parents. I'll play for both of you."

Trey's crooked smile stretched wide across his face. "What's a little rivalry between old friends, right?"

Delores, the twins Courtney could never tell apart, and their tiny blond friend offered cheers of encouragement.

Riya refused to meet anyone's gaze, training her eyes on the empty space to the right of Courtney's hip.

"Right," Courtney said. Should be a piece of cake. Courtney had practiced every day since she was four. Though Riya had tons of natural talent, she'd taken pains to hide it, suppress it even. Courtney had nothing to worry about. So what was with that nervous tickle in the pit of her stomach?

"Sure," Riya muttered, not sounding sure of anything.

"It's about to start," Trey said with boyish enthusiasm. The entire mood shifted.

"What's starting?" Riya asked, following Trey.

He turned to tell her about the upcoming silly skits, where Bob Fazio and the other staff made absolute fools of themselves. Courtney'd loved the whole thing when she was a kid, but now it seemed so stupid.

Everyone migrated toward the fire like moths to a flame and, suddenly, they were in a Taylor Swift music video for a song about summer nights. Campers laughed and flirted and licked marshmallow guts from their fingers as the fire sparked and flared in the background.

The new junior counselor, Jacob, stood in a line of counselors, his muscled arms tense across his chest, a scowl on his face. Dane shoved him forward.

Courtney hung back. Despite the amazing weather, her perfect outfit, and her newly established truce with Riya, she couldn't get into the camp spirit.

It took Colt all of three seconds to zone in on her mood—or lack thereof. He joined her, still standing in the same spot where she'd challenged Riya to the talent show. They stood side by side, watching everyone from twenty feet away.

Well, Courtney mostly watched Riya.

"I thought you two talked," he said. It sounded like an accusation.

"We did." Courtney swept her hair up and swirled it into a bun at the crown of her head, then dropped her hands, letting gravity slowly unravel the strands.

"And?"

"She said she didn't like me. I mean—you know, that way. She called the kiss a childish mistake." Courtney didn't admit she wasn't sure if Riya still liked her in *any* way. She'd changed so much in four years, while Riya had only grown kinder. Better.

"Isn't that the exact same thing you told me?" Colt asked.

Courtney nodded. "Yep, it was a mistake."

Colt made a noncommittal sound, cocking his head to the side. Courtney watched him from the corner of her eye for a few seconds. His jaw moved in a familiar way; he was literally chewing on his tongue.

"What?"

"So why aren't you happy?"

He wasn't asking a question. He was making a point.

Having a twin meant there was someone who knew your every thought. Most of the time—like when she snuck out of the house or had forgotten her lunch—it was great. But other times? It was total crap.

"She's amazing," Colt said without the admiration that usually accompanied such a phrase. He was making another point.

"She always was." The words fell from her lips like a river rushing into a waterfall.

"She's nice, smart, funny." Colt spoke with an almost clinical air. "She manages to be cute and hot at the same time, which is basically witchcraft, if you ask me."

Courtney nodded with caution. This felt like a trap. "Yep. What's your point?"

"My point is, big sis: What's not to like?"

"I don't like girls."

"Maybe not." Colt shrugged and turned to face her, bowing his head to peer directly into her eyes. "But you do like Riya Johnson. Or, at least, you did."

The hair on the back of her neck rose to attention. Courtney tried to slide her hands into her pockets, but they only went as deep as her second knuckle. Damn girl pockets.

"I don't like *any* girls," she insisted.

"Why not?"

His question caught her completely off guard. Girls never had to defend *not* liking other girls. It was the other way around; girls who liked girls had to explain themselves.

It simply wasn't done. Especially by girls who traveled the kinds of social circles she did, where there were always whispers about the family who suddenly sent their son away to boarding school or the college-age daughter who brought her "roommate" to every benefit and function.

Her mind flashed to the welcome talk, when their thighs had been pressed together and the heat of Riya's skin had scorched her awareness until that small space became the only thing that existed in the world.

Colt raised a blond eyebrow.

"Either way, it doesn't matter. She said she doesn't like me. So everything's okay now."

"Court, every bonfire we've ever had here, you've been out there." He pointed to the jumble of kids gathered around the fire. "Working the crowd, practically forcing every single boy to fall in love with you. Tonight, you're standing alone, sulking, staring at someone you swear you don't care about. That's all I'm saying."

With his mention of her staring, she sought out Riya's dark head and found it, silhouetted against the rising flames. The jocks surrounded her, everyone beaming as she told a story with wild gestures. Trey stood on her left, close, and laughing hardest of all. Blood rushed to Courtney's cheeks, heating her skin.

"Seriously, Court. You're not being yourself. Figure it out."

Courtney pulled her shoulders back and raised her head. "Nothing to figure out. Everything's perfect." She sashayed into the crowd, winking at the first boy who checked her out.

Chapter Four

Riya clenched and unclenched her jaw as she walked back to the cabins with everyone else. Six hours in this camp and Riya had pissed off her first crush and apparently signed up for her worst nightmare, but at least Colt was happy to see her. And that Trey kid seemed nice.

How had she let her parents talk her into this? She'd wanted to go to volleyball camp again, but they'd argued this was her last summer to have fun. They worried she was too serious and it was only going to get worse once she went to college, studying pre-med while — hopefully — playing college ball. There was no arguing with her parents, who were literally *the* experts on what students needed. Every year, they worked at a different school system, building or overhauling special needs programs.

At least she didn't have to help them move everything to Charlotte. Again. No matter how many times she moved, the actual act of unpacking and setting up the house always seemed like an impossible task. So much tedious work only for it to be undone in a year or two.

The group diminished as they walked, first by half as the guys took off in the opposite direction, then again as a few girls from G7B veered toward their cabin. Finally, Dee, Riya, and Courtney walked together. The other girls from their cabin had already headed in.

The silence hung thick in the air, more palpable than the humidity. Dee glanced at Courtney like she was a vampire, ready to attack at any second.

Courtney opened her mouth to speak a couple of times before finally getting words out. "You shouldn't lead him on."

"What?" Riya and Dee chimed at the same time.

"Lead who on?" Riya asked, trying to think if Dee had been flirting with anyone.

"Trey," Courtney said, meeting Riya's gaze for a fraction of a second. "He's a nice guy. Don't lead him on."

Riya tripped over an imaginary pebble. Her brow creased. "What makes you think I'm leading him on?"

Courtney rolled her eyes. "Come on, you two were flirting all night."

"And?" Riya asked. "He's cute and funny and I like talking to him." While she spoke the truth, she also relished the opportunity to show Courtney how well she was moving on without her. *See how much I don't need you?*

"He's my friend. I don't want him to get hurt. And, well." Courtney cast a glance at Dee. "I don't want to…"

"Whatever you're thinking, just spit it out."

"You like girls," Courtney whispered.

Dee pressed her lips together so hard they turned white and threw her hands up in the air. "This chick!" was all she said.

A small, single laugh rumbled Riya's lips. Dee sure had a way with words. Then another laugh escaped as she fully understood, the realization halting her steps. Poor Courtney. She really was so confused. About absolutely everything.

Courtney folded her arms across her chest, and her chin jutted out in annoyance. She spun, facing Riya. "Don't laugh at me, I'm just trying to save my friend embarrassment. You shouldn't be playing with his emotions like that."

Riya's cheeks warmed with a powerful flush. She wondered if Courtney could see it in the scattered light cast by the moon and building lights. But Riya was used to this. She'd faced assumptions like this a dozen times over the last couple of years. It, unfortunately, came with the territory.

"Courtney, I'm bi," Riya explained.

But Courtney gave her a blank look, and her head twitched. "Bi?"

"Bisexual."

Still, Courtney stared open-mouthed.

"She dates girls and boys," Dee finally clarified for her. Riya felt a rush of gratitude for her new friend. She'd told her the same thing earlier in the afternoon, and Dee simply nodded like Riya had said she liked to eat pizza.

"That's a thing?" Courtney's perfectly smooth brow creased.

"Have you been living under a rock?" Dee asked, not unkindly.

Courtney shook her head and twisted her lips. "Kinda. I guess I thought there were lesbians and straight girls and then there were girls who made out with other girls at parties to get guys' attention."

Riya bit her lip to keep from laughing again. "That's a totally different thing."

Courtney placed a hand over half her face, shaking her head. "I'm not an idiot, okay. It's just... We—I don't know anyone who is..." She waved her hand, and Dee supplied the words.

"LGB or T?"

Courtney shrugged. "Sure. None of that."

"It's fine," Riya said, really wishing the conversation could be over. Very much out of the closet, she usually didn't mind talking about her sexuality. But Courtney's full attention made her squirm. She didn't even mention that, statistically speaking, Courtney probably knew several people who weren't het. "Now you know."

Riya resumed their walk back to the cabin and the other two joined her.

Courtney still looked confused. "Do you date them at the same time? Like can you date a girl and a guy?"

Riya shook her head as she took the first step up to their cabin. "If I'm with someone, I'm with only that person. If I'm dating a guy, kissing someone else is still cheating, no matter their gender."

"Straight people don't have a monopoly on monogamy," Dee said, then shrugged. "Or playing the game, either." She swung open the door to their cabin and burst out laughing. "Looks like revenge came swift for you, newbie."

Riya pushed past her into their cabin and followed Dee's gaze to discover her duffel bag strung to the ten-foot-high wooden rafters with the same twine they'd used to tie her bunkmate's bed.

"How am I supposed to get that down?" Riya gaped at the scene. There were no bunks underneath her bag, not even close. No chairs or tables she could pull over and climb up. The other girls in the cabin prepared for bed but paused to glance at the bag and giggle or shake their heads.

"Who the hell did this?" Riya demanded.

Courtney had gone still and silent behind her. Riya turned to find those blue eyes staring straight at her.

"You're number four?" Courtney's voice was incredulous, accusatory, and fearful.

In an instant, all the clues clicked into place. The expensive luggage. Courtney's group of friends who were so obviously the popular and rich kids. Discovering they had been assigned the same cabin. *Dethrone our queen*, Trey had said.

"And you're the queen bee," Riya said.

Courtney scoffed, and Riya could practically hear the unspoken *duh*.

Her heart thudded in her chest. She'd pranked Courtney without even knowing it. And Courtney had pranked back without knowing the identity of her victim.

Shots had been fired. What had Riya started? She felt dozens of eyes on her back as all their cabin mates realized what was going on. The skin on her neck itched.

"How did you even get that up there?" Riya asked, scanning the room again in case she'd missed something.

"I have my ways. Who did you think you were pranking?"

Riya swallowed, looking to Dee for help, but not finding it. "A, um, rich bitch?"

A slow, sly smile inched across Courtney's bubble-gum-pink lips. "Well, you got that right." Her left hand went to her hip, and she clicked her tongue once. Then she declared, "Oh, this war is *so* on."

But then Riya realized something far more unsettling. For the next four weeks, Courtney Chastain, the girl Riya couldn't glance at without drooling, the first person to have ever broken Riya's heart, would be sleeping inches underneath her. There'd be no avoiding her, no matter how hard she tried. Riya swallowed and pressed her shaking hands tightly to her thighs.

"You look scared, number four," Courtney taunted. "Worried you can't take the heat?"

Riya's mouth went dry. *The prank war*, she reminded herself. Courtney was talking about the prank war. No other kind of heat.

Her mind kept flashing to the image of Courtney curled up beneath her bunk. She wondered if Courtney still slept on her left side, waist bent, left arm tucked under her head and right arm curled against her chest. Her golden hair would fan out over the pillow, and her face would relax until she resembled an artist's rendering of a sleeping angel. Then and now, Courtney was always the most beautiful when she wasn't trying to be, when she thought no one was watching.

Courtney stared at her, waiting for a reply, but Riya's mind had lost all capability for human speech. Her former best friend and first crush had mutated into a super-hot mean girl, and they had to spend the next four weeks practically sharing a bed.

Luckily, Dee jumped in. "Prepare yourself, princess." She rested her elbow on Riya's shoulder, leaning in to her. "You don't know who you're messing with."

When Courtney had been staring at her for a solid five seconds, Riya stretched a smile across her face through sheer force of will. Words remained elusive, so she nodded.

Courtney smirked.

Dee dropped her elbow and used it to nudge Riya's ribs. "I know where we can borrow a ladder to get your bag down."

"Sounds great." Riya's voice cracked over the words. With considerable effort, she turned away from Courtney and gave Dee her full attention. "I'll follow you."

. . .

Courtney woke up to her pillow vibrating. It took a few seconds of sleepy confusion to remember she'd placed her cell phone under her pillow with the alarm set. She slipped a hand underneath and turned it off, then extended her arms above her head in a luxurious stretch. The wire mesh above her bent ever so slightly, and yesterday's events came rushing back.

Riya Johnson.

Of all the bunks in all the summer camps in all the world, why did she end up in this one?

So much for the prank war being a distraction. Now Riya would occupy even more of her head space. She didn't need another reason to think about Riya all the time, but she couldn't back down from the challenge. What would people think? Courtney Chastain never backed down from anything.

As quietly as possible, Courtney grabbed her brush, some clothes, and her toiletry kit before slipping into the silent bathroom. The peace of the mountain morning before anyone else stirred calmed her. She shimmied into green tights, removed her pajama top, and slipped into a heather gray sports bra. As soon as she snapped every elastic seam into place, a soft sound behind her made her spin in place.

Rubbing her eyes and carrying a jumble of clothes and shoes, Riya stumbled into the bathroom wearing a loose tank and elastic shorts that barely covered the important parts. Her thick black hair stuck up at all angles with the left side flattened against her head. Her eyes drooped almost completely closed.

She was halfway to a stall before she noticed Courtney. Riya jumped back half a step. "Uh," she said, glancing sideways at the bathroom exit, looking like she wanted to make a run for it.

"What do you think you're doing?" Courtney asked. She wasn't waking up early to dance specifically so she could avoid Riya, but she'd considered it an unintended perk.

Riya swallowed and stared at a bathroom stall door. "I was going to go practice my serves?" It sounded like a question.

"Serves," Courtney echoed, trying to make sense of it. She took Riya in with a lingering once-over. Normally, Riya wore slightly baggy clothes, so Courtney hadn't noticed how powerful her body had become. Her skinny childhood legs had filled out with a considerable amount of muscle, her smooth, brown skin stretching over formidable thighs and shapely calves. Courtney became hyper aware of her shirtless state and snatched her dance tank, slipping it over her head.

"Like, volleyball?" She remembered Riya coming home from school late every autumn because of volleyball practice. She also remembered keeping the phone in the basement with her while she danced on those days, impatient for her call to come over.

Riya nodded. "Volleyball."

A couple seconds of silence was more than either of them could stand.

"Well, I'm done here, so it's all yours," Courtney said.

At the exact same time, Riya said, "I got a scholarship."

Courtney had started to move toward the door, but curiosity stopped her. "A scholarship?"

Riya nodded and met Courtney's gaze for a second before becoming super interested in the bathroom sink. "A fancy private school. We can't afford tuition without it, so I have to make sure my game doesn't slip. Four weeks without practice could mean the difference between my also getting a college scholarship and…" She shook her head. "I'm sorry, I don't know why I'm telling you all this. You don't care."

Courtney was surprised to realize that she did care. Or she was curious. It was hard to tell sometimes. "What happens if you don't get a college scholarship?"

Riya shrugged. A thick lock of hair tumbled down to shield the left side of her face. "I guess I'll have to take out student loans. I want to do sports medicine, so it's going to take a while. You know my parents will help where they can, but…" She trailed off.

"Yeah." Courtney understood. Even as a kid, she'd been aware of the financial differences in their families. Riya's parents were educational consultants. They'd followed their passion. Courtney's parents, on the other hand, had followed the money. And the power.

Courtney thought of her own situation and the impossible prospect of Juilliard. Her parents could definitely afford the tuition, twenty times over, but they wouldn't support anything besides their pre-arranged life plan for her. If only there were scholarships for rich girls to study dance. Yeah, right.

Riya's rich brown eyes flashed to Courtney's, and she bit her lip. "Are you going to dance?"

Courtney's eyes widened. "Hm?"

"Is that why you're up so early?"

"Oh. Yeah." Courtney'd almost forgotten.

"You're an incredible dancer, Courtney." The way Riya said it, with so much raw honesty and not a trace of self-interest, made Courtney's heart squeeze tight inside her chest. Riya gave compliments in their purest form, with no ulterior motive or envy. Courtney couldn't do that. It wasn't in her.

The genuineness of her own smile surprised her. "Thank you."

Riya nodded and turned toward the bathroom stall.

"If you can change quickly, I'll walk over with you." She didn't know what made her say it. She'd wasted enough dance time talking already.

But the way Riya's smiled blazed over her shoulder at Courtney incinerated her second thoughts.

"Just a sec." Riya scurried into the stall.

Courtney turned to check her reflection in the mirror while she waited. The rustle of clothing and whisper of cloth against skin filled the small space. Courtney fidgeted with her tank, smoothing her hands over nonexistent wrinkles. The sound of an elbow smacking the stall wall exploded like a gunshot in the silence. Riya hissed, and Courtney swallowed a chuckle. The girl was certainly no ballerina. How she played competitive volleyball with such high levels of documented clumsiness, Courtney had no idea.

A few seconds later, she staggered out of the stall, sliding her feet into tennis shoes and looking sheepish. "Sorry. Ready."

They both dropped their sleeping clothes on their bunk and tiptoed out of the cabin, attempting to mitigate the creaking door as much as possible. As they walked in silence, Riya combed her abundant black hair with her fingers, then slipped an elastic from her wrist and pulled her mane into a high, tight ponytail.

Courtney snuck sideways glances at Riya. She'd told her she didn't want to be friends. She'd told herself to stay away from her, to continue on with camp business as usual. She'd literally declared war on the girl in front of their entire cabin. And, somehow, here she was, taking a morning stroll with her. The harder Courtney pushed her away, the more the universe seemed intent on shoving them together.

"See you at breakfast?" Riya asked.

Courtney looked up to discover they'd reached the tennis and volleyball courts. The arts and crafts hut, a.k.a. her makeshift dance studio, waited on the other side of the pool.

The hopefulness imbued on Riya's features twisted something in Courtney's stomach. She'd told Riya not to lead Trey on. She should follow her own advice.

"Well, we're kinda required to sit with our cabin, so I basically have to." Courtney tried to make her tone as dismissive as possible.

When Riya's smile fell, she knew it had worked. And wished it hadn't.

"All right." Riya half turned toward the volleyball court, but she kept her gaze on Courtney as if she'd say something else. "Have a good practice."

You, too, she thought. But she didn't say anything aloud. Without a word, she turned and jogged to the arts hut to warm up her muscles.

New rule. She would not be nice to Riya Johnson. She couldn't take the way those big brown eyes looked at her afterward. Courtney'd never had a problem not being nice to someone before. Riya was no different, she told herself.

Chapter Five

Riya concentrated on keeping the heaping pile of scrambled eggs, bacon, hash browns, and toast steady on the oversize tray in her hands. Every meal, one person from each cabin was responsible for carrying the food back to their table, and Riya had been assigned the first breakfast. Lucky her. At least she wouldn't have to do it again for a while. But with her complete lack of grace, she should've been exempt.

"Excuse me." She leaned in between two chatting girls and lowered the tray to the table. Once it sat securely on the surface, she breathed a sigh of relief.

Dee waved and pointed to the open spot next to her on the bench. Riya smiled and slid into the seat.

She scanned the table as everyone started scooping food onto their plates. Most of the girls still sported pajamas and wore their hair unbrushed or pulled into messy ponytails. Courtney was nowhere to be seen. Not that she'd been looking, of course. The way Courtney brushed her off this morning made it clear she had no interest in being friends, despite their shared early-bird status. Maybe that would be easier, Riya thought. It was probably best they spent as little time together as possible.

"This is Riya," Dee announced to the girls sitting around her. "Some of you met her last night. She's a newbie, but she's cool."

Nods and small smiles answered Dee's declaration.

Two of the girls were the twins who'd been hanging around with them at the bonfire last night. "I'm Stefanie," one said before nodding to her sister. "This is Tiffany."

Riya nodded, examining them for anything that might help her tell them apart. They were both tall with athletic builds and serious faces. They had the same haircut and wore different colors of the same shirt. They didn't make it easy. Finally, she spotted it. Tiffany had a tiny rectangular scar in the center of the bridge of her nose. She hoped they didn't wear makeup.

"I'm Elise," a slender blond girl with an adorable overbite chirped. "I'm terrible at all sports, but they let me hang out with them anyway."

Riya laughed. "I'm sure you're okay."

"She's really not." Dee laughed. "We keep trying, though."

Elise shook her head slowly, but smirked.

Conversation halted when everyone had food on their plates. Riya's stomach rumbled more than it usually did in the morning. Maybe what they said about fresh mountain air was true. She shoveled a forkful of scrambled eggs into her mouth as the morning announcements began. Being the first day, it seemed there wasn't much to say. Camp Counselor Becky ran through a list of the day's available activities. Her ponytail swayed as the woman bobbed with unnatural energy.

As she chewed on crispy bacon, Riya's gaze flitted lazily about the room before landing on a familiar blond bun near the younger kids. Courtney knelt at the end of a table, chatting with an earnest-faced redheaded girl sitting with the ten-year-olds. They finished their conversation, but Courtney didn't make her way to join her cabin. She found her brother's table and swept from boy to boy, smiling and touching everyone's shoulder. Most of them followed her movement, like sunflowers to the sun.

"So, you and Courtney Chastain, huh?" Elise's voice rang high and clear, carrying over the chatter.

Riya dropped her fork on her plate. "H-huh?" she stuttered. How did Elise know? How long had Riya been staring at Courtney? Was it that obvious? Did everyone know?

"We all heard you last night," Elise clarified with a tone so innocent for someone publicly outing such a complicated relationship.

Swallowing her food, Riya's mind raced back over everything that had happened last night. There had been no one in the cafeteria when they talked. She had checked. Her heart pounded in her ears, drowning out the clanking of dishes and chatter.

Oblivious to her distress, Elise continued. "So when are you going to make the next move? It's your turn, right?"

"My turn?" Riya choked out.

"If you need help, I have some ideas," Dee added, bizarrely supportive.

The twins and Elise nodded in agreement. Riya couldn't figure out what the hell was happening.

"Dee brought an entire extra bag in preparation for pranking," Elise said. "I think it's bigger than her actual bag."

The breath whooshed out of Riya's lungs.

Right, the prank war. Of course. Riya versus Courtney. Not Riya *and* Courtney. Not like that.

Her eyes, acting entirely of their own accord, found Courtney still at Colt's table. She leaned so far into a guy named David that she might as well have sat in his lap. To say David didn't complain would be a serious understatement.

Finally, Courtney made her way toward their table, hips swaying and attitude oozing from every invisible pore.

Courtney's gaze met Riya's and the blonde cocked an eyebrow. "Got a problem?"

The girls sitting at the far end of the table giggled. Riya looked at them, her forehead wrinkling. It wasn't that funny.

Riya focused on her empty tray. Dee started singing something, but it took a few seconds for Riya to realize what it was. A laugh burst from Riya's lips as she recognized the tune.

Dee raised her voice for the most well-known line. "I got ninety-nine problems but a bitch ain't one." The twins and Elise joined her for the final five words, Elise substituting "bleep" for the curse word.

Courtney huffed and plonked down to sit on the bench, snatching a piece of bacon from her friend's plate.

Dee bumped her shoulder against Riya's, who flashed her a small smile.

"Thank you," she said, her voice unable to convey the full extent of her gratitude. Since Courtney, she hadn't made any friends who'd stick their neck out to stand up for her.

Counselors started herding campers out of the dining hall, so they dropped their plates in the designated spot and filtered out with the crowd. Younger kids skipped and shrieked about what they wanted to do first.

Riya made a detour on her way out the door. She was scooping a handful of ketchup packets when she spotted the mayonnaise next to them. Courtney *hated* mayonnaise. She'd once called it "the most disgusting substance ever invented on the entire planet." Courtney'd always been a fan of hyperbole. Riya filled her pockets with the silvery packets before walking out into the fresh mountain air.

"Riya," she heard Becky call behind her. "Courtney. Wait. I need to talk to you two."

Riya's heart pounded against her ribs. What had she done? Was she in trouble? In the seconds it took to walk back to Becky, Riya's mind was already imagining the worst. She'd be sent home on the first day. Her mother would be "disappointed."

"What's up?" Courtney said with breezy nonchalance. Riya couldn't help wondering what it would be like to have even half of the girl's self-assurance.

Becky fisted her shiny blond ponytail and ran her hand down the length of it. "I noticed y'all weren't in your beds when I woke everyone up. Where were you?"

Riya froze. It hadn't occurred to her that her early mornings would be a problem.

"Nancy said I could use the art building to dance in down times," Courtney said.

Becky pursed her lips and looked at Riya, who was having trouble controlling her breathing. She never got in trouble. She hadn't seen Becky unsmiling in the entire time she'd been at Pine Ridge, so her serious expression rendered Riya's tongue inert.

Courtney cleared her throat. "Riya was practicing volleyball. She has a scholarship, so she has to stay in top shape in order to keep it."

Becky nodded, and Riya snuck a glance at Courtney, whose forward-facing gaze didn't waver.

When Becky spoke, Riya jerked her attention back to the counselor. "It's against the rules for y'all to wander about unattended."

Riya frowned. Losing her morning practices would be a disaster.

"I understand that, Becky," Courtney said.

Riya's heart plummeted. She hadn't realized how much she'd been relying on Courtney to find a way around the rule.

"But is there any way we could work something out?"

Courtney said, her voice firm but respectful. "If Riya loses her scholarship, she'll have to switch schools."

Riya's jaw dropped open slightly as she turned to look at Courtney again. It reminded her of when they were kids and Courtney, knowing how completely useless Riya was in a confrontation of any kind, would defend Riya from whatever stupid boy was trying to make her cry. But this time, Courtney had no reason to defend Riya. She could've just argued her own case and left Riya to fend for herself.

"The ability to practice in the morning is really important to both our futures," Courtney concluded. She'd hate to hear it, but Riya saw a little bit of her mother in Courtney at that moment.

Becky pulled her lips tight as she considered. "Okay, but you two have to walk with each other, both to and from the practices. No wandering about on your own. And check in with me when you get back to the cabin. Deal?"

"Thanks for understanding, Becky," Courtney said with a soft smile. "I appreciate it."

When Courtney elbowed Riya, she realized she hadn't uttered a single word the entire conversation.

"Thank you, Becky," Riya said. "Thanks so much."

Becky waved off her gratitude, and the two girls headed for the door.

"Thank you, Courtney," Riya murmured.

She stared up at her, but Courtney didn't return eye contact. Instead, she barreled ahead, racing Riya to the door and disappearing into the early morning sunshine.

Riya stared after her for a few seconds before walking outside, where she found Trey waiting for her. "Riya!" he called over a gaggle of shorter kids and jogged up to her.

His amber eyes sparkled like the lake behind him, reflecting the morning sun. "What are you doing first?"

Riya glanced back at her new friends, and Dee raised an

eyebrow at her, accompanied by a knowing smirk.

"Oh, hiking. Luckily," she said, motioning at the lake. "It's perfect weather for it."

"Awesome. That's on my schedule, too." Trey smiled at her, and it brightened everything around them. "Don't leave without me, okay?"

Riya nodded. "Wouldn't dream of it."

"Okay," Trey said, but then didn't make a move to walk away.

"Okay," Riya echoed.

After a beat of silence, they both laughed. "See you," Riya said before turning to catch up with Dee.

The older girls had a long trek to their cabin, almost to the other side of the lake, since the younger cabins were closer to the office. They were closer to the pool and courts, which separated the oldest girl cabins from the oldest boy cabins, so it was a decent trade-off. On the walk back, they teased Riya about Trey.

"He's sooo cute," Elise crooned.

Riya smiled. "I guess."

"Yeah, he's cute," Dee chimed in. "But he's got nothing on Colt." Her face softened and took on a dreamy quality.

Stefanie and Tiffany laughed a laugh as identical as their faces.

"Girl, you've been crushing on him since you stopped believing boys had cooties," Tiffany said.

"It's our last year, Dee. It's now or never," Stefanie added.

"You like Colt?" Riya elbowed Dee. "Why didn't you tell me?"

Dee shrugged and, for the first time since Riya'd met her, lowered her eyes shyly. "Everyone has a crush on Colt."

"Really?" Riya asked, checking with the other girls, who nodded.

"Pretty much," Elise confirmed.

Riya'd never thought of him that way, not once. "I don't."

Dee glanced across the lake on their left toward the guys' cabins. "I'm content to crush from afar."

Elise rolled her eyes. "Not this again."

"What again?" Riya asked.

Dee wouldn't meet her eyes, so she looked at Elise for an explanation.

Elise held up finger quotes. "Guys like Colt don't like girls like me," she said, rolling her eyes even bigger than before.

Though Riya understood what she meant, she scoffed at the idea. Colt wasn't exactly like "guys like Colt."

"I think you'd be surprised," Riya encouraged. "Besides, what have you got to lose? This is the last summer you're both going to be here. If he's not interested, you'll never have to see him again."

Dee fell quiet, and they passed two more cabins before she spoke. "You were friends when you were younger. What do you know about him?"

Riya grinned and grabbed Dee's hand, squeezing it. "Everything! What do you want to know?"

• • •

Courtney was washing her hair before bedtime when she heard snatches of conversation over the stall door coming from the sink area. She recognized Riya's voice. When Delores said Trey's name, Courtney shifted toward the curtain to hear better.

"I like him," Riya said. "He's cute and funny and nice."

Courtney's gut twisted painfully. Those two were all wrong for each other. They'd realize it sooner or later. Hopefully sooner.

Delores laughed. "You've said that, like, a hundred times. Don't you have anything further to report?"

A beat of silence followed. She hoped Riya was shaking her head.

"Has he kissed you yet?" Delores's voice was teasing.

Something popped in the shower, and Courtney realized she'd squeezed her conditioner bottle until the top had snapped open. She froze, listening for a sign that they heard.

"No," Riya said. She didn't sound eager for that to change. "It's too early, don't you think?"

Courtney's stomach untied itself.

"The twins are cool," Riya said.

Courtney's ears twitched at the t-word. She leaned as close as she dared to the curtain to catch every word.

"Yeah," Delores agreed.

Courtney's brow twisted in confusion. She'd been positive Delores didn't care for her, and the feeling was mutual.

"They're incredible players," Riya said.

Players? Courtney was still trying to figure out what exactly that meant when Riya spoke again.

"Is Tiffany always so serious, though?"

Oh, the other twins. They *were* great volleyball players. Damn it. Courtney wondered if they'd ever get around to talking about her. Why would they, though? Delores and Courtney had been going to the same camp for three years and had never exchanged more than a couple words. And a couple pranks.

Courtney shook her head, recognizing her own crazy. Eavesdropping on girls she didn't give a rat's ass about. She was supposed to be ignoring Riya, not covertly listening to her inane conversations.

She squeezed a large glop of conditioner into her palm and began to work it through her strands. A strange, almost sour smell filled the air around her. Courtney froze midstroke. She stepped back from the stream of water, sniffing it. Just a slight metallic smell, like usual.

But when she turned to inspect the shower stall, the scent increased. Slowly, she raised her hands to her face. Conditioner coated her hands in uneven splotches. She inhaled.

And gagged.

Mayonnaise.

Mayonnaise soaking into her hair and her skin. Mayonnaise dripping down her naked body. Mayonnaise sliding down to her butt crack.

Courtney gagged again.

"Riya!" she shouted.

Riya and Dee broke into hysterical laughter. It faded as they retreated to the bunks.

Courtney's face flushed hot with anger. Riya Johnson knew exactly how she felt about mayonnaise. She'd used her prior knowledge to concoct one of Courtney's worst nightmares. That bitch.

Frantically, Courtney thrust her hands under the running water and rubbed at the foul gelatinous goo coating her hands.

Every time she moved, she got a fresh waft of disgusting condiment smell. She squeezed out a giant handful of shampoo and washed the oily mess from her hair. She still smelled it, though. It was in her pores and clinging to her hair. She washed her hair twice more and scrubbed her entire body with a loofah until her skin was pink.

When Courtney was sure she'd gotten rid of all the repulsive gunk, she stood under the water until it ran cold, then shut off the tap. She slipped a hand outside of the curtain to grab the towel she'd hung on the hook. Her fingers struck cold tile. Courtney stuck her head out, searching for her towel. Maybe it had fallen on the floor, or maybe she'd put it on the next stall over.

But her towel was nowhere to be seen. Realization struck like a hammer. This was a double prank.

"Riya Johnson!" Courtney called.

Riya and Delores appeared at the end of the shower stalls. A couple of other girls joined behind them seconds later. Courtney's green-and-blue-striped towel was hooked around Riya's index finger and tossed over her shoulder.

"What?" Riya said, voice dripping with false innocence.

The girls behind her giggled.

"Give me my towel." The words were deep and threatening, a growl.

More faces appeared behind Riya until Courtney was sure every girl in their cabin stood in the bathroom with nothing but a thin sheet of vinyl between them and her naked body. It was too early for Becky to have returned from whatever the counselors did every night in the cafeteria, so the closest counselor was the one keeping watch outside the cabins and wouldn't hear her if she called for help.

Riya looked at the towel over her shoulder like she'd just realized it was there. "Oh, this?" She extended her arm.

Courtney rolled her eyes. "Give it to me."

"I say make her come get it," Delores said.

A couple of girls standing behind them voiced their agreement, but Riya froze. The smile fell from her face, and her chest rose sharply. Her gaze traced the edge of the shower curtain.

Courtney's hand slipped on the vinyl, and she took a step back.

"No. I have a better idea." Riya had recovered, but her voice wasn't as strong as it'd been seconds earlier. "I'll toss it to you."

Courtney raised her eyebrows. If she knew Riya—and she did—there was a "but" coming, or an "if." A big one.

A smirk curved one half of Riya's lips. "After you sing 'I'm a Little Teapot.'"

Courtney groaned.

This was *war.*

Chapter Six

Riya woke early again to a completely silent cabin. She'd lain still for a couple of minutes, listening for the sound of Courtney waking. The past four mornings, she and Courtney had gotten ready alongside each other in utter quiet and walked to their respective practices without trading a single word. Courtney had found a way to ignore or snark at her every other time of the day. When they hung out in a group with Colt, Courtney spoke only to her friends. Despite Colt's gallant efforts, most of her and Courtney's communication consisted of trading pranks back and forth and the resulting shouts and promises of revenge.

Not hearing any sound from Courtney's bunk, Riya shimmied down the ladder. She reached a foot to the ground and hit something sooner than expected. It rocked under her toe, then settled. She wrenched her neck around to peer at it.

Little plastic cups littered the floor around her bed. They stretched seven feet in any direction and were half filled with a dark liquid. Close to her bed, the cups were spaced too closely for Riya to slip a foot in between them.

Strange shapes lay below the cups. Riya squinted. As her eyes adjusted, she recognized her clothing. Every piece of clothing in her dresser had been spread flat across the floor before the cups were placed. So if she messed up and knocked one over, whatever was in the cup would stain her clothes.

Pure evil.

Courtney's bed was empty. Riya looked around, but the tall blonde did not emerge from any shadows.

Riya slid onto Courtney's mattress easily. The scent of rose petals wafted up from her sheets and pillow. Riya lay flat on her stomach and picked up a cup, bringing it to her face and sniffing. A sugary, fruity scent greeted her.

She sloshed the red liquid around the cup until inspiration struck. She scooted to the head of the bed and poured the liquid from the cup in her hand into another one until it was full. There was still a small amount left in the cup, so she poured that into another cup. She smiled.

"Should've filled them all the way up," she murmured. Though how Courtney had placed so many cups in the dark without waking anyone, Riya could not imagine. How early had she gotten up? Had she slept at all?

Riya worked slowly, pouring three cups from the foot of the bed into four cups near the head. She carved a foot-wide path into the maze until she couldn't reach out far enough to grab another cup.

Carefully, focusing on every movement, she stepped down into the hole she'd made and squatted. She continued clearing a path in front of her, pouring the liquid into cups on each side.

When she'd finally reached the edge of the cups, she pumped both fists into the air, resisting the urge to cheer. Around her, campers still slept, but a soft giggle sounded from the bathroom area.

"Courtney?" Riya whispered.

The girl's willowy frame sauntered toward her. She just stood there, arms crossed, as Riya finished cleaning up the mess.

"Hurry up and change so we can head out," Courtney said.

Riya changed, and they walked out the cabin door thirty minutes late. Clouds obscured the sun's position low in the eastern sky.

"You kinda pranked yourself, too, with this one," Riya pointed out.

Courtney shrugged. "Worth it. I'm a little disappointed you didn't spill anything, though. I thought for sure…" She trailed off.

It was the most she'd said to Riya in four days. Luckily, there was so much at camp to distract her from Courtney's aggressive brand of frigidity that she'd barely noticed the chill in the air every time they had to share the same space.

A thinning mist danced across the lake's glass surface. They walked past the other girls' cabin in uncompanionable silence. The camp was so quiet at this hour it was easy to pretend they were the only two there.

Their sustained muteness weighed heavily on Riya, until the pressure finally pushed words out of her mouth.

"Courtney," Riya began, voice cracking. "Thanks for the other day. Arguing with Becky on my behalf."

Another shrug. "It worked out for me."

"It reminded me of that one time, at the mall, with the boy from my school." Riya released the smallest of chuckles. "Remember?"

Riya heard a puff of breath that could have been a laugh and took it as encouragement.

"I think he might have peed his pants, he was so scared of you." Riya laughed.

Courtney hadn't raised her voice—she never did—or

threatened him, just calmly detailed everything that would happen to him in prison after her parents sued him for harassment.

Riya risked a glance at Courtney and discovered her lips twisted, trying to contain a smile.

"He ran away and knocked all the bags out of that man's hand," Riya said, pausing between words to stifle her giggles.

Courtney burst out laughing. "Mr. Baskwill," she mocked. Her laugh sounded high and clear in the cool mountain air.

The man had turned out to be their principal, shopping with his wife.

Courtney leaned forward, doubling over with laughter. "Oh, he deserved it, though. Calling someone the 'r' word is just wrong, especially when it's my—" Courtney sobered abruptly. "My friend."

A pang of regret traveled from Riya's stomach outward into every limb. In her head, there were two Courtneys, and she couldn't reconcile the disparities. Which one was real? The one who'd defended her as a kid and argued on her behalf yesterday and laughed with her ten seconds ago? Or the one who left her hanging in a tree with a broken heart and now acted like she could not care an ounce less? Riya didn't even know if it was worth it to find out the answer.

"Do you want to go to Penn State?" Courtney asked, gesturing to Riya's T-shirt. It was heather gray with PENN STATE emblazoned in dark blue.

Riya stared down at her shirt, which she'd grabbed blindly from the pile of clothes she'd scooped off the floor into her dresser. She suppressed the surge of hope and excitement that welled up at the sight of the bold letters with practiced constraint. "I guess."

Courtney turned to look at her. Her blue eyes looked gray in the cloud-filtered sunlight. "You don't sound very sure."

"I mean," Riya began, clasping her hands together behind

her back to keep herself from fidgeting. "I'd love to go there. I've talked to their coach. But I have to go where I can get a scholarship, and they may not want me enough."

"Why the hell not?" Courtney's words were defensive, but her tone was soft.

"They're consistently one of the top ten teams in the NCAA, *and* they have great academics. They can take their pick of setters." She'd been so careful the past year to not get her hopes up.

Shaking her head, Courtney frowned, then sighed.

"What?"

"You sell yourself too short. You always have." She tugged on her high ponytail, then wrapped the long strands around her hand. "Never mind."

"You have no idea how good—or not—I am at volleyball. You haven't so much as said a word to me in four years." Riya felt the uneasy warmth of a flush creeping up her cheeks.

"I've been watching the games here, remember?" Courtney said.

As if Riya could forget Courtney lying out next to the court every other day sporting the skimpiest bikinis the camp would allow.

Riya squeezed her hands together. "Those games are… recreational, at best."

"You got that scholarship, so you must be good." Courtney's words came quick and low. "You always get whatever you decide you want. Plus, you're good at everything."

Riya already had her rebuttal prepared, but Courtney's last statement halted her words. Good at everything? "I am not good at everything. Hardly anything. I can't even use the bathroom without giving myself a bruise."

Courtney laughed a brisk, tight laugh. She pointed to her right, where the short path leading to the volleyball court lay.

"All I'm saying is, if you decide you want it enough, you'll find a way to make it yours." She paused. "Talk to you tomorrow morning."

Riya stood there for a couple of seconds, watching Courtney jog the short rest of the way to the arts hut. She glanced down at the logo on her T-shirt, then back at Courtney, then back at her shirt. A ghost of a smile pulled at the corner of her mouth before she shook her head to dispel it, reminding herself whom she was dealing with. One minute of conversation didn't make up for years of iciness. And it didn't change the fact that Courtney was now a seasoned heartbreaker who felt nothing for her.

Riya wiped away the last remnants of her smile and turned away, jogging to the volleyball court.

Colt and Trey stood outside the cafeteria when Riya walked up with the rest of her bunk.

"Good morning, ladies," Trey said, before turning his full attention on Riya. "How are you liking Pine Ridge so far?"

His mess of curls flopped unevenly to one side, shading half of his face so that one eye looked golden in the morning sun and the other looked brown.

She smiled at him. "Can't complain."

"Yeah." His smile had a weight to it. "Me neither."

He walked her to her table, lingering to chat. Riya kept one eye on the door, half hoping Courtney would walk in and catch them flirting. Riya wanted Courtney to see how happy she could be without her. But breakfast was starting. Becky gave Trey some serious side-eye, so he retreated to his table. Courtney still hadn't arrived.

Riya had already taken several bites of her amazing blueberry French toast casserole when Courtney finally strolled through the door of the cafeteria. She'd slipped a roomy lavender dolman sweater over her tights. The flush on her cheeks was natural, but the long, fluttering lashes had a little help from mascara. While everyone around her lumbered through the room like zombies, she moved with a supreme grace, like she floated across the floor instead of walked.

She slid easily into the seat her friends had saved for her on the other side of the table without even glancing at Riya.

Once again too chipper for the morning, Becky was running through the day's upcoming activity schedule.

"And tonight's activity is one of my personal favorites," Becky gushed, pausing to squeeze her shoulders together and give them an open-mouthed smile. "Capture the flag!"

At their tables, the ten- to eleven-year-old crowd cheered at hearing the same news. Riya thought it could be fun, but then she caught the expressions on her tablemates' faces.

"Why do you guys look like she just told us we're going to square dance tonight?" Riya asked.

"Square dancing would be more fun," Elise said, and Riya couldn't tell if she actually thought square dancing would be fun or if she hated capture the flag that much.

"They don't separate out the age groups," Tiffany explained. "And the younger kids run around screaming with no strategy or game plan. The teams are too big. It's chaos."

Stefanie nodded in agreement. "Last year we tried to leave to play cards, but the counselors guilted us into staying."

"But they always have good snacks on Capture the Flag night," Elise pointed out.

On the walk back to their cabin, Riya told her friends about Courtney's prank.

"Oh, the bug juice prank!" Elise exclaimed. "I always thought that one was fun until I realized how wasteful it is, with all those plastic cups."

"So what's next?" Tiffany asked.

"I've got some ideas," Dee offered.

"Don't you worry," Riya said. "I've got one all ready for her. Just don't get up early to use the bathroom tomorrow morning, okay?"

The girls giggled.

"I knew the moment we met, you'd fit right in," Dee said, slapping Riya on the back.

Riya couldn't stop the grin that spread across her face. It'd only been a week at camp, but Riya'd never had a group of friends like these girls at any of her schools. Of course she'd had friends before—she wasn't entirely incapable of talking to people, just mostly—but not like this. Not the kind of friends you know have your back, no matter what. Not the kind of friends she'd miss when she moved on again.

. . .

Dewey, the pool lifeguard, blew the whistle signaling the end of the swimming session. Lunch time, finally. Courtney's stomach growled with impudence. That's what she got for being late to breakfast. Kids groaned and splashed toward the pool ladders and stairs.

Bridget, lying next to her on a towel, stretched her arms above her head. Her legs and stomach, like Courtney's, glistened from a mixture of sweat and tanning oil. She and her friend had gone with a very loose definition of "swimming" during the activity period.

They'd been assigned different cabins this year, and Courtney found herself missing Bridget terribly over the past week. This was their fifth summer as camp friends, though they never talked during the school year besides exchanging occasional likes on Instagram. Bridget wasn't super deep or even very nice, but she was easy. She didn't ask complicated questions or force thoughtful conversation. And, despite her perfect body—with incredible C-cups, wide, swaying hips, and a flat stomach between—Courtney had never felt the tiniest hint of attraction toward her. What she'd told her brother was true, she assured herself as she stared at Bridget's smooth skin without a single prick of desire. She didn't like girls.

"So, you're going after David this time, huh?" Bridget asked, too casual to be as uninterested as she sounded.

Courtney shrugged. "He's cute enough." Though she'd gotten the same thrill she always got when she managed to snag a boy on her hook, she felt nothing for David himself. No spark, despite squeezing the biceps she'd heard other girls swoon over. "Why?"

Bridget swept to her feet and started straightening out her crumpled dress. Her gold bikini glittered in the sun. She didn't look at Courtney. "No reason."

"Uh-huh." Courtney wasn't buying it. She stood up and stepped into her shorts.

Bridget pulled the dress over her head. She sighed. "He was on my short list. Which has gotten shorter the last couple of days."

Courtney laughed. "I'm not attached. I'll back off if you want." She tugged on her pale blue tank.

Bridget ceased fidgeting with her dress and looked at Courtney, gauging her reaction. "Oh, would you?"

"Yeah, of course," Courtney said. "Anything for my camp BFF." Not that she cared either way. David was a beautiful distraction, but she appreciated his six-pack and dimples the same way she appreciated Monet paintings. She acknowledged they were pretty, but she didn't experience an emotional response to them. Not like she did with Picasso paintings.

Bridget beamed, tossing her brunette waves over her shoulder. "Besties," she sang.

They began the long walk to the dining hall.

"Wish you could sit with me at lunch." Bridget pouted. "Everyone in my cabin this year is so basic."

"Me, too. My cabin isn't any better."

"Oh, I heard you have a new nemesis this year." Bridget perked up at the prospect of gossip. "Gimme all the deets."

Courtney groaned a complaint. Why did everyone insist on talking to her about Riya all the time? "Just some girl in my cabin. She helped Delores prank me before she even knew who I was, then I did the same. Now, it seems, we're enemies."

Bridget shot some serious side-eye at Courtney's tone. "I thought you loved prank wars."

Courtney shrugged, knowing Bridget would accept it and let it go. She didn't want to explain why this time was different. She didn't want this time to be different at all.

"Well, if you need any help, let me know. Even if you just need a lookout. It must be tough being in the same cabin with her, knowing she could walk in at any time."

And that was, quite possibly, the most insightful thing Bridget had ever said to her, and the girl didn't even know it. "Thanks, Bridge."

Courtney switched the topic to David's abs, and Bridget picked up the conversation, running full-speed with it until they walked into the dining hall.

Riya and Trey stood in an aisle halfway between their two tables, talking. Their cheeks were flushed. Riya had pulled her hair into a side braid and loose strands stuck out, caressing her shoulder. Courtney walked right by them without so much as a nod, but neither of them seemed to notice her presence. Riya was laughing, hand fisted over her mouth, her brown eyes wide with amusement.

Ugh, Courtney wished she could grab a plate and sit with her brother. But that was strictly against the rules. She'd gotten away with not sitting at her table at a couple breakfasts, but only because she'd moved from table to table, never lingering too long in one spot. Plus, it had left her starving, and she needed the energy. She planned to dance during the post-lunch quiet time.

Courtney slumped into a spot on the end, as far away as possible from where the other pair of twins and the loud-mouthed Elise sat, knowing Riya would sit with them again. Across the room, her brother met her gaze and raised an eyebrow, smirking. The bastard.

She sat up straight, raising her nose high into the air, and pulled on a practiced mask of self-importance.

Courtney smiled at Jenna and Kanda, her two friends in her cabin this year. Luck of the draw, she'd ended up in a cabin with so many jocks. Jenna and Kanda were both sweet and—even though they played sports at camp—were definitely not jocks.

Riya finally joined their table when Delores delivered the tray of food. Courtney watched her scoop heaps of mac and cheese onto her plate, then top it with veggies and a thin slice of turkey, mixing it all together. Courtney decided to try it the same way. When she looked up from mixing the dish, she caught Riya watching her with a half smile on her face.

Courtney did not look at Riya again.

At the end of what felt like a four-hour lunch, Colt sauntered up to her.

"What are you doing this afternoon?" he said.

She raised one shoulder, then dropped it. "I don't know. I'm trying to figure out how many times Dewey will let me lie by the pool and call it swimming."

Colt laughed. "Probably depends on which bikini you're wearing."

She made a face. "Gross."

"Come on, Court. Dewey's a nice guy."

"Yeah, okay."

Colt rolled his eyes. "You're terrible. Anyway, I was wondering if you'd join me for singing. David apparently has plans to help Bridget with…something? I'm not really sure. So I need someone to keep the beat."

He did, huh? Wow, Bridget moved fast. Courtney was an awful percussionist if it required more than two drums, but she could bang a bongo with the best of them.

"Sure, why not." Courtney sounded bored, but she loved playing with her brother, even if she'd never say that out loud.

"You're a goddess," he said, making a mockery of a bow.

"I know."

. . .

Instead of dancing like she'd planned, Courtney had spent the rest period rehearsing with Colt in the cafeteria. She did dance for a couple minutes, when Colt busted out some classic Tchaikovsky. One of the counselors technically taught the singing session, but Colt had been more-or-less running it going on three summers now.

They'd been discussing which song they should do for the talent competition when campers started filtering in. Campers of any age could join the class. Pairs and trios of each age group joined over the next couple of minutes until about twenty kids filled the room. Colt was telling them all to come closer when a solo figure strolled through the door.

Riya.

Jesus, Courtney couldn't catch a break.

Colt burst into a smile. "Glad you could make it," he said to her.

Riya glanced at Courtney before looking at Colt. She twisted the fingers of both hands together. "I figured if I'm going to make a fool out of myself in front of everyone at the talent show, I should practice, like you said."

Colt had done this on purpose. He'd asked both of them to come without letting them know the other would be there. She glared at the side of his head, but either he didn't notice or he didn't care.

Riya took a seat two tables back. When she tried to fold her arms together, she whacked her elbow on the edge of the table. Her face contorted with pain, and she rubbed at her funny bone.

Courtney should've known better. Colt had encouraged Riya to sing in the talent show, offering to play for her. Of course he'd convince her to join the class. She considered storming out in protest until she spotted little Olivia sitting in the front row, staring at her. For some misguided reason, the little redhead looked up to her, and Courtney didn't want to set a bad example.

So she sat there as every person in the class sang one verse of a song of their choosing, so Colt could ascertain their progress. Lastly, he called Riya by name.

"Riya's joined us a little late," Colt said. "She's shy, so let's give her a warm welcome."

She stood up, her gaze flicking to Courtney like a nervous tick.

"I thought this was group singing?" Riya's voice went really high at the end.

"It's only this once," Colt promised. "Just so I can see where you're at."

Riya leaned over to scratch her knee. "I don't know what to sing," she said.

"Anything will do," Colt said.

Her eyes scanned the room as though she were looking for inspiration. One more peek at Courtney and she took a deep breath, closing her eyes as she drew oxygen into her lungs.

"You are so beautiful, to me," she began to sing.

At first, her voice came out shaky and unsure, but Colt smiled and nodded, motioning for her to breathe from her belly.

She stood straighter, raising her chest. Her gaze drifted until she stared out a side window. "You are so beautiful, to me."

Riya's voice had always been lovely, but now there was something else, a soulful quality that hadn't been there before. It crackled like an old record in just the right spots. Colt didn't stop her when he'd heard what he needed to make his assessment, like he had for every other camper.

By the third line, Courtney'd forgotten herself and stared, as transfixed as every other person in the room. Riya's brown-to-pink ombré lips wrapped around each word like a penitent caress, sending shivers down the skin of Courtney's back.

She wasn't sure when Riya had turned her head and met Courtney's gaze. She wasn't sure why she hadn't turned away, either. But when Riya's voice slid over the final line like caramel in a luxe chocolate commercial, Courtney noticed the heat warming her cheeks. Riya's buttery voice combined with her tender mahogany eyes made Courtney grateful for the sturdy chair supporting her.

Even though they hadn't applauded for anyone else, the entire class clapped when Riya finished singing. Courtney didn't applaud. She stared, blinking.

"That was wonderful, Riya." Colt turned his head to catch his sister's attention. "What do you think, Courtney?"

She swallowed, nodding. "Incredible."

Riya's chest rose slowly as she pressed her lips together, a smile pulling at the corners. "Thank you." She dropped to her seat.

Before Colt continued with the class, Courtney spied the satisfied smirk on his face, and she had the sneaking suspicion she'd been set up.

Chapter Seven

When Riya had first been told of the scheduled nap time, she thought it was silly, but that day she'd laid down on her bunk after lunch and immediately passed out. She'd only woken in time to go to the next activity session thanks to Elise's shrill voice calling for Stefanie and Tiffany to hurry up. That girl sure did pack a lot of decibels into such a small frame.

That was why she'd walked in to the singing session a little late. With all eyes on her and no crowd to get lost in, it was also the only reason she didn't immediately turn and walk out as soon as she saw Courtney at the front of the room. Bailing would create a bigger spectacle than staying and toughing out the session. Or so she'd thought. Until Colt had made her sing solo. Her skin still crawled at the thought of singing in front of all those other people.

But the way Courtney'd looked at her as she sang, when she called her "incredible," had left Riya in a stupor for the rest of the day. Courtney did not like her, she kept reminding herself. But there were moments when she thought, just maybe… And those moments were the worst ones, when she lowered her defenses and pictured a different future than the inescapable one.

Though she'd taken the afternoon class on distinguishing between edible and poisonous plants, Riya hoped nobody's life depended on that knowledge because she remembered none of it. At least she knew the pasta primavera sitting untouched on the plate before her was safe to eat.

"You okay?" Dee hissed in her ear.

Riya shook her head as if she could shake her thoughts loose. "Just having a rough day."

"Really?" Elise chimed in. "Because I heard you did so well in singing that everyone in the room instantly fell in love with you."

Riya breathed a small laugh without smiling. "People exaggerate." She changed the subject. "So what are we going to do tonight?"

"We could TP the boys' cabins," Dee suggested.

Tiffany shook her head. "There will be too many people running around for us to get away with it."

"We could play cards again," Elise said. "I have ten pounds of candy in the bottom of my dresser."

The twins teased her about her candy addiction. Dee kept getting prank ideas shot down by Tiffany, who Riya was beginning to believe never agreed to participate in any of Dee's pranks.

Before she knew it, the girls had pulled her from her funk, and they spilled out into the setting sunlight drunk on laughter.

Where they ran straight into Courtney's crew. Courtney clung to the back of some tall ebony hunk Riya hadn't yet had the pleasure of meeting, her legs wrapped around his hips, piggy-back style. Bridget, the pretty brunette Courtney spent most of her free time with, sat similarly upon the back of the same David Courtney'd been flirting with at breakfast the other day. The girls' shrieks of laughter rang through the air as the boys chased each other in a circle.

"Let's race," David called to his friend.

Trey popped up next to Riya. "Great timing. I need a jockey." He swept in front of Riya and bent his knees, holding his arms up to catch her. Apparently, this was a thing.

Riya glanced at her friends, who grinned back at her. *What the hey?* She jumped onto Trey's back.

"We're ready!" Trey announced.

"We have a challenger!" the boy carrying Courtney said.

Riya wrapped her arms around Trey's chest, holding tight. He gripped her wrists, laughing.

"Come on, Blondie." Stefanie grabbed Elise's hand, tugging her behind her. "Let's embarrass these boys."

Yelping, Elise leapt onto Stefanie's back. The sound echoed clear across the lake.

"Oh-ho-ho," David shouted. "And we have a girl-on-girl team. Better grab a jockey, Chastain."

Tiffany took three steps back, attempting to blend in with the shadows. Dee watched with an awkward smile. Colt cast about, searching for someone he knew.

Riya recognized the moment for the excellent opportunity it was. "Colt," she called, jerking her head in her friend's direction. "Grab Dee."

Colt spun to find Dee, freezing for a second.

"Oh, no," Dee said, waving her hand back and forth. "I couldn't."

But Colt bounded to Dee in three steps, taking her hand and twirling her around until she stared at his back. "Let's go, Delores," he said. "I've seen you on the paddleboard. You've got the best balance out here."

Dee flashed a wide-eyed look at Riya, who gave her a thumbs-up. Dee grasped Colt's shoulders, and he bent down, catching her easily and hefting her up to rest on his hips.

Grinning, she said, "My friends call me Dee."

Colt turned his head to smile at her. "All right, Dee. Let's kick some ass."

She whooped in agreement.

"Who's the dude carrying Courtney?" Riya whispered in Trey's ear. *And where the hell did he come from?* she didn't add.

She felt his shoulders move under her arms.

"Her new flavor of the week. It's his first summer here. I think his name's Derek?"

"You don't sound sure."

"Why bother learning their names? She'll dump him in a couple of days, anyway." He didn't sound like he approved. "Poor guy doesn't know what he's in for."

Riya wondered if Trey had ever been one of Courtney's flavors of the week but decided she didn't really want to know.

"Last one to the volleyball court is a rotten egg," David called.

With that, their herd of piggyback riders sprang into action. Riya bounced up and down, holding on to Trey for dear life. Derek and Courtney took an early lead, his long legs giving him an immediate advantage. Other campers cleared the path for them, the guys' shouts and girls' screams announcing their arrival like a train horn barreling through a small town. The gravel crunched under their feet, pebbles skittering off the path. True to form, Elise's shrieks drowned out all the others.

They passed the halfway point, the G4 cabins.

A couple feet ahead of them, Dee turned her head, and Riya caught the look of pure joy etched across her face, transformed to a glowing bronze by the golden setting sun. She looked beautiful, fierce and strong and happy—and incredibly stable. Colt had been telling the truth; she had great balance. The pair surged forward, separating from the pack, gaining on Derek and Courtney.

Seeing his friend pull ahead of him, David grunted and shifted into high gear.

Trey turned to Stefanie running alongside him. "Can't let 'em win that easily," he said.

Stefanie nodded. "Hold on, Chels."

They caught up with David, passing him as Colt caught up with Derek just past Riya's cabin. Almost there. Colt and Dee ran neck-in-neck with Courtney and her new fling.

"Go, Dee, go!" Riya called.

Twenty feet from the volleyball court, Dee pulled tightly against Colt, and he surged ahead. The two collapsed onto the soft sand seconds before Courtney and Derek crossed the out-of-bounds rope. Riya and Trey stumbled over the line at the exact same time as Stefanie and Elise.

"Third place!" Elise yelled, reaching over to high five Riya.

David came panting behind them, dropping to his knees in the sand. Bridget was the only one not laughing.

Dee lay flat on her back next to Colt, both of them catching their breath.

"We make a great team, Delor— Dee." He gave her a side-hug.

Dee's smile stretched so wide, Riya thought she might never be able to frown again. Riya slid down Trey's back, stretching her toes into the sand.

"No fair!" Derek laughed, looking at Colt. "You have a freaking ninja as a jockey."

Colt scoffed. "Dude, you have the most graceful ballerina east of the Mississippi."

Derek turned to Courtney, who pressed up against his side. "You're a ballerina?"

She smiled demurely, peering at him through her lashes. "I'm lots of things."

Riya wondered what in the world they had talked about if he didn't know about the most important thing in Courtney's life. *Maybe they don't talk at all*, an evil voice inside her head suggested.

"What did we win?" Dee asked, sitting up and brushing sand from her shoulders.

Courtney's friends laughed.

"Nothing," David said. "Bragging rights."

"What kind of race is that?" Stefanie complained.

"Jocks," Bridget said with a roll of her eyes.

"Right?" Courtney said.

With their muscles, David and Derek were obviously athletes, and Colt was no stranger to recreational sports. She wondered why guys got to be athletic but not singled out, while the girls earned an extra label for it. Maybe because popular guys were expected to play sports—but what were popular girls expected to do? Stand on the sidelines and look cute? None of it seemed very fair for anyone. She wondered if her new school would be different. They were basically giving her money for being good at a sport, so she had high hopes for a different social order.

Colt jumped to his feet and held a hand out for Dee. "You, my victorious teammate, have won a chocolate chip cookie, my treat."

After a second's hesitation, Dee took Colt's offered hand and let him pull her up. She raised a skeptical eyebrow. "The cookies are free."

Colt laughed. "First round's on me, then!"

They walked the rest of the way to the bonfire field, from where the Capture the Flag game would be launched. Trays of cookies, brownies, and little bottles of water covered two six-foot tables. Her friends raided the table as if they hadn't eaten all day. She picked at a brownie, trying to ignore how Courtney hadn't even glanced at her since she'd left the singing class. She didn't want to notice; she didn't want to care. But if she'd ever been able to tell her brain what to ignore and her heart what not to care for, Courtney wouldn't hate her in the first place.

Dee and Colt stood slightly apart from the group, lost in conversation. Dee tossed her head back, her dark waves bouncing as she shook with laughter. Colt nudged her with his elbow, grimacing exaggeratedly.

"I swear!" Riya heard him say.

Riya caught Dee's eye and gave her a smile that said, *See?*

She tried to listen to Tiffany, Stefanie, and Elise discuss theoretical Capture the Flag strategies, but Courtney kept touching Derek's biceps and stomach. It was all she could do not to gag. A buzzing sounded in her ears.

The counselors separated them into groups by cabin numbers, cabins with A's on one side and B's on the other. In her group were her friends, Courtney, David, Derek, and a whole bunch of people she didn't know.

"We're on the same team," Courtney squealed to Derek, leaning her shoulder into his chest.

Riya resisted rolling her eyes, but just barely.

Standing next to her, Dee stared at Colt on the other side of the field. Trey waved when he saw them watching.

"I don't feel so great," Riya whispered to Dee. "I'm going to head back now."

"Okay, I'll go with you."

"No, I'll tell Becky I'm sick. You should stay, see if you can catch up with Colt."

Her friend's eyes darted across the field to him. "You sure?"

"Yeah." Riya smirked. "Capture the Colt."

Dee's tan face flushed pink. "You're a dork," she said, but she was laughing.

...

When Courtney's alarm shook her awake the next morning, she stretched and smiled. Last night had been perfect. She and Derek used the excuse of looking for the flag to take a nice moonlit stroll through the forest surrounding the camp. At one point, they'd heard weepy music drifting to them through the trees and ran away, laughing. She decided Derek was the strong, silent type. That was to say, he didn't talk much. So Courtney carried the conversation, which was fine by her.

When she'd returned, Riya dozed soundly on the top bunk. She hadn't noticed when she'd left, though she didn't remember seeing her after the whistle blew. Actively ignoring Riya required her to be constantly aware of Riya and where she stood at all times. It was exhausting and counterintuitive.

Courtney slipped her clothes from her dresser and made her way silently to the bathroom. She'd set her alarm ten minutes earlier this time, hoping to avoid the awkwardness of the last couple of days. She could wait for Riya on the front porch instead of sharing their uncomfortable morning ritual again. Tossing her clothes over the door of the stall, she pulled down her shorts and plopped on the toilet seat.

Tiny popping sounds exploded in the quiet and something cool and viscous hit her legs. "What the–?" She looked down to find thick red goo splashed across her legs, her shorts, the floor, and the lower half of the bathroom partitions. Panicked, Courtney performed a quick inventory of her body, checking for a bleeding injury. Her hand smeared the gunk across her calves. The stall looked like a scene from a cheap slasher film. But, no, she felt fine. Plus, the red was too bright and thick for blood.

A tangy smell filled the air.

Ketchup!

She sprang to her feet and twirled around, then lifted the

seat. Ruptured ketchup packets tumbled to the floor and into the bowl of the toilet.

That girl and her condiments.

Courtney groaned. She'd dropped her guard, and now she had to wash everything before escaping to the arts hut. At least she'd been wearing black pajama shorts, and not her trademark white ones. But then she laughed. This was a new one. And brilliant in its simplicity. She'd have to come up with something great as retaliation.

She turned a shower on and rinsed the ketchup from her shorts and legs.

When she was wiping down the stall floor, Riya stumbled into the bathroom. She'd braided her hair before bed, but wide locks had escaped to frame her face in soft black wisps. Her eyes weren't fully open yet, and her expression reminded Courtney of a newborn kitten.

"You're up early," Riya said before spotting Courtney on her hands and knees, wet, pink paper towels in her right hand. She froze, then her eyes went wide, and she slapped a hand to her mouth to stifle her chuckles. "I almost forgot."

Courtney mustered her best scowl and went back to wiping at the ketchup remnants. "You could have ruined my clothes."

"Yeah, because the bug juice wouldn't have stained my clothes." Riya's voice crackled with sarcasm.

Courtney jerked her head up to glare at Riya, who met her gaze with an unwavering stare. Confidence, defiance. This was new. Courtney kind of liked it.

As Riya changed and brushed her hair, Courtney took extra time to make sure she removed every trace of ketchup from the stall walls. Not that she actually cared about how clean it was, but it gave her something to do.

"Ready?" Riya's voice came from much closer than expected.

Courtney craned her neck to stare up at Riya, who stood just outside the stall door. She'd wound her long, dark hair into a fresh, tight French braid and wore another pair of those curve-hugging short shorts with an oversized DHS Volleyball shirt that said, IT'S IN YOUR HEART, OR IT'S IN YOUR FACE!

Courtney hopped to her feet and brushed past Riya, flinging dirty paper towels into the trash on her way out the door. Outside, Riya's feet scuffled on the steps as her shorter legs attempted to catch up with Courtney.

Riya squeaked.

Courtney spun and everything seemed to slow down. Riya's arms pinwheeled as she tried to catch herself with small, stumbling steps. Courtney lunged forward and reached out her arms, catching Riya's shoulders with both hands. Riya's momentum carried her forward two more steps, and she halted inches from Courtney.

Riya's lips parted as she heaved deep, panicked breaths. The rhythmic rushes of air grazed Courtney's face, smelling of sweet mint. Riya raised her big brown eyes to meet Courtney's. Her cheeks flushed garnet against her bronze skin.

"Thank you," Riya said, her voice rasping deep in her throat.

Courtney's heart pounded painfully against her ribs, and she told herself it was just adrenaline, not the knowledge that her lips hovered a twitch away from Riya's. The way her breath seemed to be trapped in her throat had nothing to do with the way Riya's eyes flashed to Courtney's lips every other second.

Courtney's hands grew clammy against Riya's hot shoulders, which was why she realized she still held them. Courtney yanked her hands back and, much to her surprise, loosed a bark of half-panicked laughter.

Riya answered with a small laugh. Courtney blinked hard, clearing her thoughts.

"How in the world do you play elite volleyball when you can't walk down stairs without tripping?" Courtney asked.

Riya's blush deepened. "I've walked down those stairs at least four times without tripping."

"Four?" Courtney laughed as she resumed walking toward the volleyball court. "Does that mean you've tripped the other twenty times?"

"Um," was all Riya said. She stared at her feet.

"Do you fall on the court?" asked Riya.

Riya giggled. "Everyone falls in volleyball. We roll and jump to our feet. Plus, we're wearing kneepads so it doesn't really hurt. Not to mention, I'm focused when I'm on the court. Walking around, I...I get distracted."

Courtney looked at Riya, wondering what possibly could have distracted her that morning, but she continued staring at her feet. Riya drew her bottom lip between her teeth and chewed on it.

In the silence that followed, Courtney scanned the mountains surrounding them. It was a clear, crisp morning, and the air felt warmer than the last couple of days. Birds of prey soared high before diving down to disappear in the treetops.

Riya broke the silence. "Where do you want to go? For college, I mean. Do you have an idea?"

Courtney sighed. "My parents want me to go to Harvard or Yale, like they did."

Riya turned her head and examined Courtney's face. "You don't sound too excited for what sounds like some incredible opportunities."

Courtney shrugged. "Doesn't really matter."

Riya's lips twisted as she thought. "Yesterday you told me that I can do whatever I want to do. Maybe you should take some of your own advice?"

Courtney shook her head. "It's different for me."

"Well, yeah." Riya scoffed. "You're Courtney Chastain. You have *everything* a girl could want."

"That's not true," Courtney said. Riya just didn't realize the pressures and expectations set on "Courtney Chastain."

"Really?" Riya was starting to sound angry. "You have money. You can actually carry on a conversation with anyone without stuttering or tripping over your own feet. You're graceful and beautiful with perfect hair and flawless skin. Plus, you're crazy smart, even though you don't want anyone to know it."

Courtney's heart fluttered when Riya said "beautiful," but it broke out into a salsa rhythm when she called her "smart."

Riya continued, unaware of Courtney's reaction to her words. Her tone grew harsher. "So what, exactly, do you *not* have?"

Courtney knew the answer right away. "Freedom," she said.

Riya pursed her lips. "You're as free as you decide to be."

Riya didn't understand. Courtney had so much to lose and she wasn't strong, not like Riya was.

Riya stopped walking, and Courtney realized they'd reached the volleyball court. The two stood still for several seconds.

"Anyway, thanks for saving me from smashing my face in," Riya said.

Courtney shrugged. "Anytime."

Riya laughed. "I really don't fall *that* often."

. . .

Courtney was squeezing every extra minute out of her practice time when someone strolled through the door of the art hut. She jumped back and shrieked. Colt stood just inside the doorway.

His eyes went wide. "Jumpy?"

Courtney half-heartedly punched his shoulder. "You shouldn't scare a girl like that."

He searched her face. "You don't normally scare so easily."

"Riya got me this morning. I guess I'm still a little on edge."

"Got you?" He stepped aside so she could enter the hut.

Courtney raised her foot onto a table and leaned forward into a hamstring stretch. "We're in a prank war. It's a long story."

"Long story," Colt echoed, sounding skeptical. "We've been at camp for a couple of days."

Courtney ignored the implications in his tone. "What are you doing here?"

"Oh!" His head jerked up. He smiled. "I need to tell you something."

"Riya's parents called, and she has to go home right away?" Courtney said, switching legs.

Colt stopped. "What? No. What?" He frowned.

"Wishful thinking."

"I like having her here. We're catching up. Our friends like her. And you said everything was okay. Nothing to figure out, remember?"

She met her brother's eyes. "Wishful thinking?"

"Oh, Court," he crooned.

"It's fine, really. I don't even talk to her during the day." For some reason, she didn't want to mention their early morning talks. They felt too private, isolated from everything else.

Colt looked like he might hug her, so she dropped her leg and bent at the waist, touching the floor with her fingertips. She could hold everything in as long as no one gave her any sympathy. She had this obnoxious habit: when she teetered on the edge of tears, the tiniest act of compassion opened the floodgates.

"Everyone knows that 'fine' is universal girl-code for definitely not okay," Colt said. "And how can you not talk to her when you're in the same cabin?"

"More than that. We share a bunk bed," Courtney muttered.

"You share a bed?" He raised his voice, getting all brother-protective on her. "Do you want me to talk to Fozzie Bear? I'm sure he'd switch your cabin."

She jolted to her full height. "Absolutely not. I can handle it." She couldn't have anyone thinking otherwise, especially Riya. She couldn't give Riya any reason to think there was something *to* handle.

He held up his hands as if he faced a wild bear. "Okay, okay."

Satisfied, Courtney lowered into a lunge, stretching her calf.

"But you should talk to her," Colt said.

The boy would just not let it go.

"You wanted to tell me something?" she reminded him, changing the subject yet again.

Colt remained quiet. Courtney raised her arms over her head, then lowered her left, staring down the length of her arm at him.

His expression drew in on itself. "You're not going to like it."

"Spill it." It was too early to tread through his mitigation. They both needed to get to breakfast.

"I think I like Dee," he said.

Courtney's forehead creased as she tried to figure out who Dee was. "Oh, Delores?"

Colt nodded.

"Like, *like*. In that way?"

"Yep."

"Huh."

"That's it?" He sounded relieved.

"She doesn't seem like your type, but if that works for you. Why do you think I'd be upset?"

"Isn't she basically your sworn enemy?"

Courtney laughed. "What, because of the pranks from the last two summers? It's not that big of a deal."

Colt twisted his lips and cocked his head. "Okay."

His confusion didn't surprise her. She'd made a big deal out of getting pranked in the past, throwing a fit, demanding the counselors do something about it—though never giving them the information they'd need to do so.

"But?" Colt asked.

But. Colt had never pursued anyone at summer camp. That was Courtney's deal. Every other summer, she'd kissed at least three boys by now. What held her back this year? She knew only one thing was different, but there was no way Riya's presence should or would have such an impact on Courtney's love life. Courtney had done a great job of totally ignoring her, after all.

"Good thing it's just summer camp," she said instead. "Because Mom and Dad would hate her."

Colt shrugged. "They don't get a vote."

"How can you be so blasé about it?" Her shoulders tensed just thinking about her parents' reactions. Colt was a great son, adored by their parents. Courtney couldn't figure out how he got away with so casually defying them.

"Why do you put so much stock into what they think? It's your life."

It didn't feel like it, hadn't in years. The only thing she had of her own was ballet. And soon, that would be gone, too.

Weird that Colt and Riya had told her basically the same thing that morning. She raised a suspicious eyebrow. "Did you talk to Riya today?"

Colt shook his head, brow twitched in confusion. "No, but *you* should." He started toward the door, then stopped, turning to face his sister. "Don't be so scared of her."

Her spine stiffened. "I'm not scared." But the way her heart sped up at the mere prospect exposed her lie, at least to herself.

His half smile provoked her. "Prove it."

"Okay, I'll talk to her, if I have a chance."

"Today," he insisted. "Talk to her today."

Chapter Eight

At lunch, her friends kept bursting out in laughter at Riya's early morning prank. "Courtney," they kept saying. "Courtney. Courtney. Courtney." Riya didn't want to hear her name any more. With every repetition, she saw Courtney leaning into Derek, Courtney sitting on Derek's lap in between sessions, disappearing with Derek during quiet time. She shouldn't care. She told herself the pangs of jealousy were leftover feelings from four years ago. Remnants of what she'd felt when she still didn't quite understand who she was.

"What movie are they playing tonight?" Riya asked.

Tiffany and Stefanie took over the conversation, granting Riya relief from the reprise.

"Definitely a horror," Tiffany said.

"No way," Stefanie said. "Probably a superhero movie."

Everyone launched into a discussion about their favorite movies. Riya was surprised to learn that Tiffany—quiet, serious Tiffany—was a sucker for cheesy rom-coms. Stefanie gagged as her twin listed off her favorites and countered with her favorite action flicks. Elise shyly admitted to an undying love of science fiction and fantasy.

"I'm a huge nerd!" she declared. Riya liked the way she said it, mostly casual with a hint of pride.

"Everyone's going to volleyball, right?" Dee asked.

For the first time that day, Riya felt true excitement. The twins were great players, and Riya couldn't wait to volley with them again. She just had to suffer through one of the artsy sessions before she could get back on the court. Riya'd never thought about it before, but now that she was required to do some kind of craft or art every day, she was definitely not even remotely right-brained. Every after-lunch session was dedicated to arts, probably to keep any of the campers from losing their lunch.

She'd settled on leather stamping, mainly because she liked Nancy more than the counselors teaching the other sessions.

As early as Nancy would let her leave the class, she headed straight for the court to get some extra practice in during the transition time, before anyone else showed. Dee volunteered to join her, claiming she was too nervous to do anything else. They'd said hello in passing a couple times that morning, but Colt promised her he'd come to the volleyball session.

They served the same ball back and forth for a couple minutes, then passed the ball over the net for a while longer. Dee had solid basic skills but lacked the control and instinct that came with playing regularly. She, unlike Riya, was a natural athlete. Bodily kinesthetic intelligence was the term. Riya had none of it.

When they both glistened with sweat, they sat on the side of the court, feet stretched out between them, rolling the ball back and forth.

After a minute of companionable silence, Dee spat out a question. "So what's the deal with you and Courtney Chastain?"

Riya raised her eyebrows, shook her head, and shrugged. She raised her hands, then dropped them.

"You're squirming," Dee pointed out, smirking. "Don't pretend like there's nothing. The vibe between you two is weird. You leave early together every morning."

Riya admired Dee's directness. Not at the exact moment, precisely, but she did admire it in general. So she disclosed everything. It felt good to get the whole story out in the open. Someone to talk things through when endless obsessive thought got her nowhere would be a welcome change.

"You want to know what I think?" Dee asked.

Riya squinted at her. "Maybe?"

Dee snickered before growing serious. "She likes you. And it terrifies her."

Sensation swelled in Riya's chest. Riya thought in silence for several seconds. If Dee was right… No, she couldn't open her mind to that possibility. Riya didn't even know if she really liked this new, more jaded Courtney, and everything would be so much easier if neither of them cared. "No way," she said. "I make her uncomfortable."

"The truth always makes people uncomfortable. Especially people like her."

"People like her?" Riya knew everyone at Pine Ridge had a very different opinion of Courtney than she did, and many of them didn't like her or were scared of her.

"She's an American princess. Someone like us starts dating a girl, not many people even blink these days, but Courtney? Everyone would talk. Some of them would pick on her, try to embarrass her. And that would be nothing compared to what she'd face at home."

Riya had experienced almost no resistance the first time she publicly dated a girl, besides gross comments from guys who tried to make it all about them. Granted, they'd both been athletes and not the first girl-girl relationship at their school. She didn't even think about it, she'd been so wrapped up in her feelings for Astrid that everything seemed perfectly natural. Her parents had always been open on the topic of sex, and they'd been the first ones to use the b-word. It wasn't until they moved last year that she realized how easy her coming out had been, compared to many. That's also when she realized that "coming out" wasn't an event, but a never-ending process. Riya kept her hair long and wore dresses, so everyone—sometimes, even, the girl she harbored a crush on—assumed she was straight.

Dee was right; dating a girl wouldn't be so uneventful for Courtney Chastain. Assuming she wanted to, of course. And an assumption based on a thirteen-year-old's kiss four years ago was not a sound one.

Riya nudged Dee's foot with hers. "How'd you get so good at this queer stuff?"

Dee shrugged. "My older brother's gay, maybe genderqueer. He's working it out. It's tough for a gay Puerto Rican dude living in Tennessee, you know? So I got really involved in the community. So many people are ready to tell their stories to someone who'll listen and not judge. Listening's easy. I'm getting better at the not-judging part."

"That's really cool."

Other students trickled onto the court. Dee and Riya started a bump circle with them, warming up until the session officially started. Tiffany, Stefanie, and Elise walked up, but Elise laid a blanket on the ground about fifteen feet from the court. Colt, David, Derek, and Courtney arrived together along with Courtney's friend Bridget. Since breakfast, Courtney's hair had been freed of its bun, and it tumbled around her shoulders, glinting in the sunlight.

Courtney and Bridget placed towels on the ground within a couple feet of the net post closest to the forest. They'd done this for every volleyball day so far, but never so close.

"You really should move back, Courtney," Colt said.

She shimmied her shoulders. "I want to be close to the action."

He rolled his eyes and joined the warm-up scrimmage. "Your funeral."

Becky walked to the edge of the court, her ponytail swinging for all it was worth, and watched for a minute. Riya felt Courtney's closeness like static on her skin, her pores tingling with awareness. Finally, Becky blew her whistle.

"Good afternoon, everyone!" she chirped. "These teams look good, so how about we just start a game."

There were six players to a side. Though that's how many played on a court, it was too many for sand. Riya reminded herself that this was recreational volleyball and ordered her competitive side to take a back seat. Dee, Tiffany, and two boys and a girl she didn't really know were on Riya's team. The girl was named Jenna and moved quickly but had terrible control, each hit shanking off in a wild direction. Derek, David, Stefanie, Colt, and two other girls squared off against them. The game began.

Becky fancied herself a referee but obviously didn't know the difference between a carry and a clean hit, so she was basically a scorekeeper and line judge. Half of the players were pretty terrible, slapping at the ball with open hands or letting it fall at their feet. David thought he was awesome, but…not so much. Every time he touched the ball, it rose no higher than his forehead, then he yelled at whoever stood next to him for not saving it.

Most of the others, like Dee, Derek, and Colt, were decent and kept the game going. Every time Courtney cheered for Derek or Colt, Riya's muscles tensed, and she willed herself to stay focused. As usual, Tiffany and Stefanie were incredible. They moved on the court like opposing forces of nature. The confidence they lacked in social situations detonated the volleyball court. Elise burst into applause when the twins went head-to-head, regardless of the victor.

Riya was finally getting into the rhythm of the game when Courtney slapped her hands together and whooped, celebrating Derek's perfectly positioned tip. Riya's shoulders burned with the memory of those same hands pressed against her skin earlier that morning. Courtney had been so close Riya could see the detailed texture of Courtney's cotton candy lips. Her legs nearly went weak with the flashback.

"Ready!" Dee called just a little too loudly.

Riya broke from her reverie to find her friend staring directly at her, her lips twisted and one eyebrow raised.

"Ready," Riya echoed.

Riya's team won easily, twenty-one to thirteen.

"Rematch!" David called.

Everyone gulped down a quick drink of water from bottles scattered around the edge of the court. By then, all the boys were shirtless and most of the girls had stripped down to bathing suit tops. Riya wore a red sports bra.

Stefanie took control of her team, placing Derek and Colt—by far, the fastest players—on each side of David to cover him. She pulled Kanda, a Thai girl who could bump set but not much else, to stand next to her.

Three points into the second game, Courtney stood, raising her arms to the sky in a lingering stretch. She shimmied out of her shorts, then crossed her arms, gripping the hemline of her shirt, and tugged it over her head so slowly Riya thought someone had hit the slow-mo button on her life. The sky-blue bikini hung low on her hips, which narrowed to a slim, muscled stomach as the shirt rose higher. Riya's heart galloped in her chest.

"Service," Derek called, and Riya ripped her attention back to the game just in time to receive his serve. She bumped it over the net, setting Stefanie up for a disastrous quick hit.

When the ball slammed into the ground, Tiffany turned to Riya with a disapproving look.

"Sorry," Riya said.

But then, her gaze found Courtney again, who'd finally escaped the shirt, sitting on her towel, rubbing sunscreen on her long, slender arms.

Derek must have called service, but Riya didn't hear it. Dee passed the serve, and it landed on the sand, halfway between Tiffany and Riya. Tiffany, who'd been fully expecting Riya to give her another great set, glared at her with a raised eyebrow.

Riya mumbled another apology. Dee laughed, which drew a confused look from Tiffany.

Dee came up under the guise of giving Riya an encouraging low five. "You're staring," she whispered.

"But, Jesus, can you blame me?"

Dee clicked her tongue, shaking her head.

When Courtney smoothed the lotion down the length of her legs, Riya became the worst player on her team. Jenna carried more weight than she did.

"Get it together!" Tiffany called after her ninth error.

She tried and failed, repeatedly. Even when she wasn't looking at Courtney, the girl shone in her peripheral vision, demanding attention.

Finally, Courtney stopped smoothing glossy liquid over her incredible dancer's body and laid flat on the towel, removing her from Riya's constant line of sight. But, by then, it was too late. Her team lost twenty-one to eighteen.

Everyone smacked hands underneath the net.

"Way to make it interesting, campers!" Becky said.

"Tie-breaker to fifteen," Tiffany said, her tone brooking no argument.

"Yep," Stefanie said, a glint in her eye.

"Oh, okay," Becky said, unsure. "Yeah."

Riya felt a little sorry for Becky. She leaned over and whispered, "Rally scoring, win by two."

Becky gave her a small smile. So adorable. She repeated Riya's words, calling them out to all the players.

The third game transformed the atmosphere. Even the less competitive players dove into the sand and sprinted out of bounds to save balls. There was something about a tie-breaker that brought out the best in players. They traded points, no team gaining more than a two-point lead at any time. The play was so intense, Riya almost forgot about Courtney's tiny bikini. She could almost ignore the way the sun glistened off Courtney's skin. Almost.

"Eighteen to seventeen," Becky announced, bouncing on her toes, signaling for Dee to serve the ball.

Riya stood center front with Tiffany next to her, a setter's happy spot. This was their chance to finish the game. Derek returned Dee's serve on the first hit, making Stefanie grunt with frustration. Riya groaned internally when the ball flew straight at Jenna. The girl hit the ball with a single extended forearm, closing her eyes as it impacted her skin. To Riya's surprise, it floated in a high arc, heading only a couple of feet out of bounds.

"Mine!" Riya sprang forward, crossing in front of Tiffany, parallel to the net. Tiffany pulled her arms back to give Riya space. Riya tracked the ball against the blue sky, instinctively calculating its trajectory versus hers. She squatted low and stretched her right arm out, fist closed, swinging slightly. The ball bounced off her fist and flew backward toward the court.

Then she tripped on the out-of-bounds rope, arms flailing, feet kicking up sand. She stumbled for what felt like minutes. Her knees fell on a towel, and her momentum carried her forward. Her arms caught her half a second before she would've collided, full-body, with Courtney Chastain. Her chest barely brushed Courtney's, setting her skin ablaze.

Courtney's eyes flew open, then focused slowly, the pupils shrinking to make more room for sapphire blue. Riya hovered inches over Courtney's glistening body. Her mouth went dry.

Courtney's lips parted as her gaze drifted down to Riya's arms, then further down to Riya's heaving chest, returning to settle on Riya's lips. Riya froze as memories from four years ago filled her mind. She could almost feel Courtney's slender fingers tracing circles on the back of her neck, the warmth of her knees pressing into Riya's thighs. The smell of coconut filled Riya's nostrils.

"You don't fall *that* often, huh?" Courtney murmured, a sleepy smirk on her face.

Behind them, she heard Tiffany roar in triumph.

"Ugh," Bridget scoffed. "Klutz, much?"

Belatedly, Courtney's face twisted into a mask of contempt. "Get off me!" she said, much louder.

Riya scrambled off of Courtney, falling butt-first into the sand and mumbling her apologies.

Tiffany yanked her up by her armpit. "Awesome save!" She gave Riya a sideways squeeze and held her other hand up for a high five.

Riya stared at it before raising her hand to smack it.

Becky's whistle blew erratically. "Nineteen-seventeen! Nineteen-seventeen!"

Tiffany hauled her back to the court, where her teammates gave her enthusiastic high fives. Riya tossed a glance over her shoulder.

Courtney was staring directly at her, mouth slightly parted and forehead creased in confusion.

• • •

When she had been younger, Courtney thought watching a movie under the stars was just about the coolest thing ever.

For years, it'd been her favorite thing about camp. They only held the movie nights in the field if there was zero percent chance of rain for the night. Otherwise, they'd be in the cafeteria.

She lay back on the grass, her head resting on Derek's thigh. She sipped from a juice bottle David passed her, filled with something more potent than juice. A superhero movie played on the pop-up screen, but she'd seen it when it played in theaters, so she only half paid attention.

Derek's long fingers caressed her hair. It felt nice. He was nice.

She was glad she'd decided to check out the woodworking class for the first time ever the other day, or else she might not have noticed him. Bridget had whined and begged her to join her at the pool again, but Courtney needed some time to herself. She never imagined she'd find a tall, dark drink of water to distract her. He was new this year and not in her brother's cabin. Fresh meat.

Movement on her right caught her attention. Someone sat up, shifting their position, and Courtney recognized Riya's silhouette. Despite her brother's insistence, she hadn't spoken to her today, not once. Not even when Riya'd fallen on top of her during the volleyball game. Courtney'd been drifting off to sleep, so when she opened her eyes, she'd thought it was a dream. Riya floated over her, wisps of her hair soaked with sweat, ragged breaths pushing her chest against Courtney's. Then Bridget spoke, jarring her awake.

Courtney forced out a breath.

Riya sat on her left, Trey on Riya's other side. Colt and Delores sat on Courtney's right. Beyond Riya, the other twins and the loud-mouthed blonde lounged, lazily tossing popcorn at each other. Since when did these two groups sit together on movie night? Since when did they mix at all? Most of them had been coming for years and never exchanged more than casual pleasantries. Now—what?—they were friends?

She'd heard people talk about how at summer camp, people made friends with people they'd never look twice at in the real world. Courtney had always thought that was true of her and Bridget, but this was beyond irregular.

Trey raised his arm, placing it over Riya's shoulders, pulling her in to his side. Riya adjusted her legs and her knee grazed Courtney's hip.

Riya jerked back like she'd accidentally touched fire.

Courtney gulped several mouthfuls of the not-juice—vodka with a splash of orange juice for color—then grimaced at the taste. She usually didn't drink much, if any. At parties back home, she'd clutch a red cup full of soda and no one was ever the wiser. And she hated how it made her thoughts burst out of her mouth, no matter how uncool.

Just for tonight, she told herself. She'd done so well ignoring Riya today. She deserved a little something to take the edge off. Tomorrow would be easier. Maybe then she could look at Riya without focusing on her lips, without her pulse beating in her throat.

Beside her, Riya wouldn't stop moving. Every other minute, she readjusted her position, her limbs bumping and brushing Courtney like a needy cat. Courtney wasn't usually the type to be bothered by people touching her, but every touch from Riya was like a livewire to her awareness.

The bottle emptied before the movie finished. Courtney didn't notice until Colt picked it up, then shook it at her, raising his eyebrow. A couple drops rattled against the plastic walls.

When the movie finished, everyone stood up slowly and lingered, chatting. Derek stood first, then pulled Courtney to her feet. She swayed, and he caught her with an arm around her waist. Lying down, she hadn't felt a thing from the vodka, but now she realized: she was drunk. Way drunk. She recognized the feeling from the one night she'd been peer-pressured into taking shots.

Across the circle composed of her long-time camp friends and her sworn enemies, Trey put his arm around Riya's waist. When Riya turned her face toward Trey's, Courtney looked to Derek.

"Wanna go for a walk?" she asked, tracing slow circles on his muscular back with her fingers.

Derek's smile lit the night. "Where?"

"Anywhere."

Derek nodded, and Courtney tossed a lazy hand toward her friends. "Catch y'all later," she murmured before leading Derek away.

They walked aimlessly. Courtney grabbed Derek's hand, mainly to steady her path. Her head spun in the quiet of the night.

Courtney broke the silence. "So what do you do for fun, besides woodworking?"

"The usual," Derek said. "Hanging out. Video games."

She asked him a couple more questions, and he answered all of them without using a single complete sentence. Before they stepped foot on the long dock, she was already bored with him. That was not a good sign. It usually took a couple of days, at least.

Courtney thought about the talks she'd been sharing in the mornings with Riya. Those blew this one out of the water. Why couldn't Derek be more like Riya? Courtney giggled, picturing a Riya-Derek face swap.

Halfway down the dock, she decided she wanted to sit down. So she did, without warning. She was too warm, so she dropped her feet into the lake. The cool, dark liquid soothed her omnipresent blisters and bruises. Everything was pretty about a ballerina, except her feet.

Derek paused, staring down at her with his lips slightly

parted. "Okay." He sat next to her.

Courtney gripped the edges of the boards beneath her butt and held tight. Even though she knew the dock was secured into the lake bed, she felt the rocking motion of a boat under her. She locked her gaze onto a light in a window across the lake until it blazed in her vision, steady and still.

Warmth enveloped her bare shoulders, and she realized Derek had put his arm around her.

She sighed. His touch meant nothing to her. His underarm was moist from sweat. She wrinkled her nose. Moist. She hated that word. And now she had underarm sweat on her shoulder.

Courtney rolled her shoulders, shrugging Derek's arm off. He raised an eyebrow at her, and she giggled.

His forehead wrinkled, and the moonlight cast shadows in the creases. "I…I'm confused."

"Sorry." She shrugged. "I'm just not interested." She marveled at how easily the truth formed itself into words, slipping out of her mouth as if they had a mind of their own.

Courtney braced for whatever was about to come. A lot of boys didn't take being brushed off well, especially when she'd just spent an entire movie in their lap.

"But you were?"

Though Courtney searched for it, she didn't find bitterness or hostility in his tone. Her shoulders drooped.

"I'm sorry," she said. "You're sweet and crazy hot. I thought you could help me forget someone else." She became convinced that vodka doubled as a truth serum.

"Ah." Derek smacked his lips. "But it's not working."

"Nope."

"That's not a very nice thing to do," he said.

So you can *speak in complete sentences.* She wasn't sure if she said that part out loud. "I'm not a very nice girl."

Derek stared out over the lake, considering her statement. "We all do wrong things for the right reasons."

"Not me. I do everything for the wrong reasons."

Derek offered her a sad smile. "I think you're a nice girl. You're just confused."

"You're half right."

"It's weird," he said, twisting his lips as he thought. "It's easier to talk to you now that I know you're not interested in me. Before, I was so scared of saying the wrong thing."

Courtney nodded once before deciding that was a terrible idea. It took a count of four before the world stopped moving. "I can be intimidating." Everyone seemed to be scared of her. Except Riya.

"Ha!" He barked out a single laugh. "True. Plus, I'm a nerd back home. Girls like you don't talk to me, ever."

"You are *not* a nerd," she said, eyes trailing over his toned arms and the way his soft T-shirt clung to his stomach, hinting at the sculpted abs she and Bridget had whispered about during the volleyball game.

"Why in the world would anyone claim to be a geek when he wasn't?"

"To get girls?"

Derek laughed so long and so hard that she worried he might never breathe normally again.

"What's so funny? Geek chic is so in right now."

He laughed even harder, wrapping a hand around his stomach. The movement drew her attention, and she looked closer at his shirt. What she'd thought was Arabic writing stretched across his chest under "No place like" written in English.

"What does your shirt say?"

His gaze dropped to his chest, and he smiled liked he'd just won an argument. "These are the glyphs on the DHD representing the chevrons needed to travel back to Earth, i.e. home."

"Huh?" She recognized about half of those words.

"*Stargate*?"

Courtney shook her head.

"It's a TV show. That nerds watch."

"I'll take your word for it."

He leaned back on his hands and stared up at the sky. He stared for so long, Courtney thought she should check out what had kept his attention. She tried to lean back on her arms, but they felt too weak to hold her. She dropped to the deck, lying flat on her back with her hands cushioning her head.

"Whoa, there." Derek examined her face. "You okay? That was like six shots you drank."

"Fine," she said, before the sky took her words away.

Living in the city, it was easy to forget how many stars twinkled every night. Between the smog, the buildings, and the streetlights, Courtney was lucky if she could make out the Big Dipper at home. But here, in a huge valley, with nothing obstructing her view and the closest town miles away, they were innumerable. Her eyes traced Scorpio, the Big Dipper, the Little Dipper, and more constellations she wasn't sure were official or just in her head. With that many stars, she could trace any shape she wanted. The longer she stared, the more stars appeared. And as long as she kept the lake out of her peripheral vision, the world didn't spin.

A soft, rhythmic *thunk* vibrated through the boards of the dock.

"Your friend's coming," Derek said. "I'm gonna go, okay?"

Unable to rip her gaze away from the millions of stars dancing before her eyes, she was vaguely aware of him standing, then walking away.

"Thanks, Derek," she called after him.

Someone sat down beside her with soft, slow movements. A cold water bottle was placed in her hand. Courtney heard the splash of feet joining hers in the water.

"I drank too much," Courtney said.

"Yeah," an unexpected voice said. "That's why I came to make sure you were okay."

Courtney's head snapped up. "Riya," she said.

· · ·

"Hey, Court." Riya cast a single glance over her shoulder. "How you feeling?"

"Great," Courtney said. "Fantastic. Excellent. Dandy." Her body was rigid, like she was trying to hold herself together by clenching every muscle in her body.

Still a terrible liar.

"Then let's get back to the cabin. It's past lights-out."

Dee said she'd cover for them, but Riya didn't know how long that would work.

"Leave me alone," Courtney said, slurring her words. "I'll come in when I'm ready. The stars are too beautiful to leave."

Or she was too drunk to stand up. In which case, there was no way Riya would leave her alone inches from a lake. Riya reclined until she lay next to Courtney, who turned out to be right. The stars were actually magnificent. A million twinkle lights on an endless expanse of deep indigo velvet. A crescent moon on the horizon cast a soft glow over everything. Worth missing curfew for.

Riya turned her head, scrutinizing Courtney's profile. "I saw Derek leaving. What happened?"

Her lips parted, closed again. She breathed out through her nose. "He's a Monet."

For some reason, that made perfect sense to Riya. "I've always been partial to Picasso."

Courtney's head swiveled to the side. She searched Riya's face. "Are you making fun of me?" Her pale blue eyes sparkled in the darkness like the light came from inside them.

Riya shook her head. "He's hot, though."

Courtney sighed. "They always are."

She didn't know what that meant, but Courtney hadn't told her to leave again yet, and she wanted to keep the peace.

"There're a lot of cute guys here." Riya wasn't sure why she took the conversation in the boy direction, but from what she'd seen, it was basically all Courtney and her best friend Bridget talked about. Seemed like a safe subject.

"Yep." Courtney turned her eyes back to the sky.

Minutes passed before either of them spoke again. So much for trying to engage Courtney in a conversation about boys. Riya was content to simply lie there, next to Courtney, staring at the sky. She kept checking to make sure Courtney hadn't fallen asleep. Her blond hair fanned out against the gray, sun-bleached wood.

Courtney broke the silence. "You and Trey are getting along really well."

Courtney bit off the ends of her words, bitterness coloring her tone. Riya wondered again if the two had dated before.

Riya chewed her lip. Guilt washed over her. "I guess."

"You guess? You two were all over each other tonight."

She hadn't thought Courtney'd noticed her at all. She laughed at herself. She literally fell on top of Courtney and the girl still managed to ignore her.

Truthfully, Trey had been all over *her* during the movie. Riya kept finding excuses to move away.

"Honestly?" Riya said. "He's great, really. Funny and smart and totally cute."

A smile pulled at the corner of Courtney's mouth when she turned again to face Riya. "But?"

Courtney's gaze lingered on Riya's. Her heart leapt into her throat, making it hard to speak. "How'd you know there was a 'but' coming?"

"I know you."

Courtney's statement hit Riya like a hard-driven spike to the face. Just like that. So matter-of-fact, no hesitation. Stunned, Riya took a couple of seconds to recover the thread of conversation.

"But," she began, pausing for effect.

Courtney giggled.

"No spark." Riya knew Courtney would understand without further explanation.

"You have to tell him." Courtney's voice filled with concern, and Riya didn't know if it was for her or for Trey.

"I did." They'd gone for a walk after the movie, purposely heading in the opposite direction of Courtney and Derek. Riya hadn't wanted to see whatever it was they were doing. Trey'd kissed her. It should have been perfect and romantic, but it was awkward and lackluster. Riya'd felt nothing. Not a single butterfly in her stomach.

Courtney raised her head to look at her. "You did?"

"I thought you knew me?" Riya teased.

"You're braver than you were." Her head clonked back to the wood.

Riya puzzled at the statement. Had she been a coward before? She hadn't thought so, but Courtney's blazing self-confidence had always been a spotlight, washing out everyone else.

"Sorry," Courtney said. "Apparently alcohol makes me super honest."

"Do you need help with that?"

Courtney didn't answer the question. "How'd he take it?"

"Better than me, I think." Riya laughed. "We've only know each other, like, a week, so no biggie." Had she really only been at Pine Ridge for a little more than a week? She felt like she'd lived a lifetime since she arrived.

"That's good."

Riya nodded. Courtney licked her lips, setting them glistening under the moonlight. Riya's mind went blank. She stared, unable to look away. If Courtney had any idea the power she held over Riya, she never let it show.

Courtney cleared her throat, and Riya tore her gaze away. She stared at the sky, no longer able to focus on the stars. Breathing deep, she closed her eyes and willed her heart to beat slower. *Friend*, she reminded herself. *Act like a friend.*

"I thought you liked that David guy?" Riya asked.

"Riya, I don't want to talk about guys with you." Courtney sounded annoyed, tired with the subject.

"Oh, thank God," Riya breathed.

Courtney laughed. "You are so adorable sometimes."

Riya swiveled her head again to find Courtney staring at her. Riya's previous heartbeat-slowing efforts proved immediately futile. Her pulse thundered through her entire body.

Adorable. That was a good thing, right? It was like cute, but better. Or she could mean adorable like a six-year-old asking too many questions at Thanksgiving.

"What are you thinking?" Courtney's eyes opened and closed ever so slowly, giving her a sexy, sultry expression. "I can see your brain turning behind those ochre eyes of yours."

Riya caught herself staring at Courtney's lips. This time, she didn't look away. "What do you mean by adorable?"

Courtney bit her lip as a smile slid across her face. If Riya didn't know better, she'd think Courtney was teasing her. "Cute. Charming. Endearing." Her left eyebrow shot up in a suggestive gesture. "Kissable."

The word struck her like a flash of lightning. Riya's entire cardiovascular system froze for a second, before jump-starting into double-time. "Courtney," she warned. "Don't do this."

"What?" Courtney asked, her voice dripping with faux innocence. "This?" She reached a hand over and stroked a single finger from Riya's knee, up to her hemline. A line of fire flared across its path.

"You are drunk," Riya reminded her. *She's drunk; she doesn't know what she's doing*, Riya reminded herself.

Courtney turned onto her side, tucking one arm under her head. "And I told you"—she raised her other arm and trailed two pink-polished fingernails up the length of Riya's arm with the lightest touch—"alcohol makes me honest."

The air Riya pulled into her lungs felt as thick as pancake syrup. Her hands fisted the material of her shorts as she resisted the urge to return Courtney's caress. "You haven't spoken to me in public except to mock me."

"Talking to you frightens me," Courtney said. "My brother was right about that at least."

Her brother? How much did he know? Neck aching, Riya rolled over on her side to face Courtney. "What are you scared of?" Riya asked. "Why do I scare you?"

Courtney's fingertips traced up from Riya's shoulder, across the heartbeat pulsing in her throat, ghosting across her jawline before tickling her lips. Riya couldn't have moved if she wanted to—and as long as Courtney touched her, she definitely didn't want to.

Courtney whispered her answer. "That what I felt that day in the tree wasn't a fluke."

Riya wasn't asthmatic, but she swore she was on the verge of an asthma attack. Or a heart attack. She'd daydreamed about this, imagined this scene in her head a hundred times, knowing it could never happen.

"That I'm not broken," Courtney added, so quietly Riya could barely make the words out.

Confusion cleared her mind for a second. "How would talking to me prove you're not broken?"

"I date a lot of guys." Courtney pulled her hand back from Riya's face but immediately grabbed Riya's hand. "I kiss a lot of guys."

Riya knew she should, but she didn't pull her hand away. Courtney's fingers felt so warm, impossibly soft. Courtney's pale skin made her seem even darker, and the contrast made Courtney's hand practically glow in the dim light. Riya made a vague sound of agreement. "So I've heard."

Courtney closed her eyes, her mascara-coated lashes fanning out against her pale cheeks. She squeezed Riya's hand, as if to say, *Stay with me. I have a point.* After a long, slow breath, Courtney said, "I feel nothing. None of the boys. No jitters, no sparks, no butterflies, none of the things you're supposed to feel." She opened her eyes. "None of the things I felt when…" Courtney trailed off, closing her eyes again.

Riya believed there were moments in every person's life, turning points that permanently altered their path. If this was one of those moments, she needed to be absolutely sure. Riya could hardly dare to hope the rest of the sentence. But she needed to know. "None of the things you felt when I kissed you."

She'd intended it to be a question, but the words were spoken without a note of uncertainty.

Eyes still closed, Courtney bit her lip and nodded ever so slightly. She squeezed Riya's hand and nodded again.

Every inch of Riya's skin felt warm and tingly. She wondered if an entire body could blush all at once. Courtney Chastain had felt something when they kissed. Jitters or sparks or butterflies—maybe all of the above.

Courtney lay still and quiet so long, Riya began to worry she'd fallen asleep. This thought reminded Riya that the girl had drank too much, of her own admission. Then she worried that her lack of sobriety nullified all of her other confessions. She was debating whether to wake Courtney up or let her sleep when she spoke again.

"Kiss me, Riya." Her voice cracked over Riya's name, and

Riya's heart cracked right along with it.

Blood roared in Riya's ears. How she wanted to give in to Courtney's demand. But, more than that, she didn't want this to be a mistake Courtney regretted when she woke up in the morning. Or, worse, something Courtney wouldn't even remember in the morning. She'd been through that before.

"I can't." The words came out raspy, like her throat tried to close up on them to keep them from escaping.

Courtney's eyes shot open. "Why? You broke things off with Trey."

It was all Riya could do not to look away. To gaze into those beseeching eyes and not kiss her was unfair. "Because you're drunk. You don't know what you're asking."

Without thinking, Riya pulled their clasped hands to her mouth and kissed the back of Courtney's hand. It was as though she were, on a base level, incapable of completely denying Courtney's request. Courtney's eyes rolled back, and she moaned softly.

"Please." Courtney squirmed closer so that mere inches separated their bodies. "Please, Riya. I need to know."

Riya's resolve nearly crumbled on the second "please." She shook her head to clear it. "It wouldn't be right. I don't want to take advantage."

Courtney tugged on their joined hands. "Take advantage, please. I may not be brave enough to ask sober."

Riya took several deep breaths, hoping for clarity and to calm her racing heart. She should just get up and walk away. Send Colt or someone else to take care of Courtney until she sobered up. But Courtney Chastain was begging her to kiss her, and that was not something she'd ever dreamed of in her wildest fantasies. How did a girl just walk away from something like that?

"Riya, listen." Courtney's voice sounded thick, as though tears choked her tongue. "When we were thirteen, you kissed me, and it rocked my world. I had never felt anything like that before and haven't since. I need to know, do you understand? I need to know if it's you or if it's me or if there's something else. I need you to kiss me, okay? I can't keep living like this. Please don't say no. I don't think I can ask again."

By the time Courtney'd finished with her plea, tears burned the corners of Riya's eyes. "Oh, Courtney," she gasped. She brought Courtney's hand closer and pressed her palm into her neck. "I have no more nos left in me."

A small smile flitted across Courtney's lips. Riya raised up, resting on her left elbow, and brushed silver strands behind Courtney's ear with her right hand. She searched Courtney's face, looking for any hint of second thoughts.

God, she was so unworldly beautiful, like a river nymph bathing in the moonlight.

Riya lowered her face to Courtney's, scarcely brushing her supple pink lips with her own, giving Courtney one last chance to recant.

A soft, blissful sound escaped Courtney's throat and Riya was done for.

She cupped Courtney's face with her right hand and pressed her lips to hers. Courtney's fingers tightened on her neck, and Courtney wiggled closer so that their bodies made intermittent contact from chest to knee.

Riya parted her lips, and Courtney mirrored the move. Her hand trailed down Courtney's arm to her elbow, then clutched at the bend in Courtney's side, pulling her even closer. Courtney's forearm sank into the space between Riya's breasts, her elbow pressing against Riya's stomach, and every nerve ending in Riya's body exploded with sensation. Tentatively, she slipped her tongue past Courtney's lips. Courtney met it with her own, letting out an honest-to-goodness moan. She tasted of popcorn and vodka.

The rest of the world disintegrated. The only thing that

existed was Courtney's tongue and Courtney's lips and Courtney's arms and the insane buzzing vibrating through Riya's entire being.

Courtney sat up and Riya followed, refusing to allow their lips to separate. Courtney placed both hands on either side of Riya's face and deepened the kiss. This time, Riya was the one to moan. Courtney flung one leg over Riya's and straddled her thighs in a move only a ballerina could pull off after drinking. Their arms and lips and tongues entangled until Riya lost all sense of time or place.

Courtney began to pull back, planting shallower and shallower kisses until her lips brushed Riya's with the lightest of touches. She rested her forehead against Riya's, a dreamlike smile on her face.

Then, suddenly, the smile vanished. "Shit," she said. "Dammit."

"What?" Riya asked, her euphoria slipping away with the gentle waves washing upon the dock's support posts. "What's wrong?"

Courtney's eyes grew wide and she frowned. "I'm gay."

Then, she spun, leaning her head over the edge of the dock, and threw up.

Chapter Nine

Razors sliced through Courtney's brain when she attempted to open her eyes. She felt around blindly for her alarm, turning it off. An entire construction crew pounded away inside her brain, twin jackhammers hammering her temples. Her stomach churned, but the last thing she wanted to do was get out of bed. She dozed off again, to be woken an hour later by the sounds of girls moving around the cabin. Moaning, Courtney tossed an arm across her eyes.

Noise in the cabin rose, then died off, leaving Courtney in blissful silence.

"How you feeling?" She knew that voice. Riya.

Courtney peeled the corner of one eye open. Riya stood next to their bunk in a white T-shirt and another pair of those wonderfully tiny shorts. In one hand, she clutched a water bottle and an oversized pair of sunglasses. A bottle of ibuprofen rattled and a bottle of the pink stuff sloshed in the other hand. The pills clacking together resounded like gunshots ricocheting in her head.

"Do you have to shake that so hard?" Courtney asked.

Riya barely restrained a grin. It stretched the corners of her mouth, forming dimples in her cheeks. As rough as she felt, there was no other sight she'd rather wake up to than that.

Riya dropped the three bottles on the bed next to Courtney before slipping the sunglasses carefully over Courtney's eyes. Without another word, she poured out a shot of Pepto and passed it to Courtney. Still lying down, Courtney tossed it back, grimacing at the chalky liquid colliding with the sticky craptastic taste in her mouth. Sitting up, she held out her hand so Riya could pour two ibuprofens from the bottle into her palm. Courtney flung the white pills to the back of her throat, taking the opened water bottle Riya offered her and swallowing.

"You're too good to me," Courtney muttered. After last night—hell, after the last four years—she believed she didn't deserve it.

"I know." Riya tossed the bottles up on the top bunk. "I bought you some extra time with Becky, but she's expecting you to be at the first activity."

Courtney slid her legs to the side of the bed, placing her bare feet flat on the cool wooden floor. Riya handed her a small piece of plastic. Courtney took it before realizing it was those dissolving strips for freshening breath. She slipped one onto her tongue, then offered Riya a guilty smile.

Riya shrugged.

"How did you get so good at treating hangovers?"

"I dated this guy…" Riya trailed off with a small wave of her hand. "That was a mistake I corrected far too late."

One side of her stomach twisted painfully. Of course Riya'd dated a guy before. Guys, even. Girls, too. She knew that. So why did picturing Riya playing doctor to some loser make her feel like she needed to throw up all over again?

"I want to go to breakfast." Courtney stood up, gripping

the top bunk for balance when her head spun. If she didn't make it to the cafeteria, people would notice, and they would definitely talk. After brushing off Derek and the imminent inevitable awkwardness, she couldn't let people think she was pining after some dude. If she was good at anything, it was pretending like she was fine when she felt terrible inside.

"Okay. Maybe brush your hair first?" Riya suggested.

Instead, Courtney tossed her head back and shook out her hair with her fingers before coiling it into a loose bun on top of her head.

A smile skimmed across Riya's lips. "How do you pull that off? When I try to do that, I look like a slob."

"And how do I look when I do it?" Courtney asked, sliding a sideways glance at Riya.

"Fishing for compliments?" Riya asked, laughing. She put a finger to her lips like she had to think about it. Courtney's eyes followed the movement, and she watched Riya's lips form around the words. "Like a model in a high-end coffee ad, padding to her all-white kitchen in a slinky robe."

Courtney giggled, then regretted it as her headache flared. "That's oddly specific."

"Stunning." Riya's voice transformed, softening to a purr. "You always look gorgeous."

Blushing, Courtney turned away, uncomfortable with the sensation. She slipped on flip-flops and walked to the door. They were several minutes late and the path was empty. The pair walked past three cabins before either of them spoke again.

Riya's hands twisted at the hem of her shirt, and she stared at her feet. "Um, so. Yeah, I'm just going to ask. Do you remember everything that happened last night?"

Heat flooded Courtney's entire body. The skin of her arms tingled. Oh yeah, she remembered.

Not trusting her voice, she nodded. But Riya wasn't

looking at her, so a couple of seconds later, she raised her head and met Courtney's eyes. "Yeah." The word grated her throat.

"And, did you…" Riya visibly swallowed, transferring her attention back to her feet. "Did you mean everything you said?" She pulled at her shirt again, exposing the wide white straps of her sports bra close to her neck.

Courtney's breath came shallow and fast. She raised a hand to push back a strand of hair and noticed it trembling. She didn't know how long she stared at it before Riya grabbed it, stopping both of their steps, and turned to face her.

"Did you mean it, Courtney?" Riya's brown eyes were impossibly big, beseeching her.

Courtney's heart pounded so hard in her chest, she thought it might echo on the mountains surrounding them. Her unsteady stomach reeled. She folded both lips in, biting down on them. Her chest expanded slowly as she filled her lungs with air, then let it all out in one puff.

She nodded. "Everything. I meant everything."

Riya bounced. A slow smile crept across her face until she sported the biggest grin Courtney'd ever seen.

Her heart fluttered against her ribcage. Pride surged in her chest, knowing she was the one who put that smile on Riya's face.

Riya bounded up on her toes and kissed her. A quick peck. It wasn't enough. Courtney slipped her arms around Riya's waist, pulling her closer. Riya's breath caught. Courtney tilted her head down, amused at being the taller one for the first time.

When their lips touched, Courtney's senses detonated. She'd thought their kiss last night had been life changing, but it was nothing compared to this, when she could feel everything, unhindered by alcohol. Her blood rushed through her veins, spurred by a new purpose.

Riya's hands gripped Courtney's arms. Electric current flowed between them everywhere their skin touched. A hunger Courtney had never felt erupted inside of her. She pressed her mouth harder against Riya's, pushing her lips apart, needing more of her. Riya moaned and leaned her body against Courtney's.

Somewhere nearby, a screen door slammed against the frame.

Courtney jumped and jerked away from Riya. She cast quick glances about, trying to figure out if anyone had seen it. Her shoulders relaxed when she realized every other camper and counselor was currently in the cafeteria for breakfast.

She'd forgotten herself. It couldn't happen again. Courtney took two quick steps back from Riya.

Riya's grin collapsed in on itself, imploding like a once-magnificent building blown to bits to make way for the newest strip mall. Her hand went limp, dropping Courtney's. "I—I'm sorry. I thought—I just thought…" Her lower lip trembled and her eyes glistened in the cloud-filtered sunlight.

Courtney felt like a heaping, steaming pile of dog shit. And not just because of the hangover. She grabbed Riya's hands so hard Riya flinched. Her face pinched in confusion.

"I meant everything I said last night," Courtney admitted, stalling until she could figure out how to put words to how she felt. "And I like you. That way. I do. Kissing you is the best thing I've ever done."

When Riya no longer seemed in immediate danger of crying, Courtney took a breath.

"But?" Riya gave her a sad half smile.

Courtney breathed a laugh. "I'm not ready. I mean, for people to know. I just found out yesterday, you know? I need time."

Riya squeezed Courtney's hands. "Of course, I'm sorry. I didn't think about that."

Courtney's shoulders collapsed with relief.

Then, as if to herself, Riya added, "I can't believe Dee was right."

Courtney stiffened. "Delores? She knows?"

Riya winced. "Kind of? She knows how I felt about you when we were younger, and she thought you might like me."

Adrenaline saturated Courtney's bloodstream. "You can't tell her. You can't tell anyone."

Riya shook her head, then nodded. "No, of course. I won't out you to anyone."

But that wasn't enough. Delores already suspected, and that girl paid attention. Pressure swelled inside her head. "We have to act the same as before."

"Before?"

"We have to pretend nothing has changed." Delores, her brother, Bridget—they would all know something was up if she suddenly started hanging out with someone she'd claimed yesterday to despise. No one could know. Not yet. Not until she figured out what all of this meant.

Riya's head started shaking and didn't stop. "We can just be friends in public," Riya pleaded. "I won't touch you and I won't tell anyone, I promise."

Courtney released Riya's hands, looking around pointedly. "No. All it will take is one little mistake or one nosy person. I can't risk it." The mere thought of someone else knowing made her limbs go numb with panic. *Did you hear?* they would say. *Courtney Chastain's a...*pause for effect... *lesbian.* Cue eyebrow waggle. She'd seen it a hundred times. Hell, she'd done it a few times herself.

"Court—" Riya reached for her, but Courtney moved away.

"No, I mean it."

"You want me to pretend, after all this time, that I still don't care about you? At all?" Riya's voice was fragile, like one wrong word would break it. The glistening in her eyes redoubled its efforts.

"If anyone else is around, yes." The coldness in her voice felt wrong. She softened her tone. "Not when we're alone, though, okay?"

Riya wiped her right eye, then her left.

"Please. I need this."

Riya took a deep breath and nodded. Pink tinged her nose and under her eyes.

Courtney smiled. She couldn't help it. "You're so damn cute when you cry."

Riya scowled and wiped furiously at her eyes, which only made then redden further. "I'm not crying."

"Thank you for taking care of me this morning," Courtney added, changing the subject. "And last night."

"Anytime. Except not—I mean, don't make a habit of that. The kissing, yes, not the drinking-too-much part." Did Riya know how adorable it was when she awkwardly rambled? "And definitely not the puking part."

Courtney grimaced. Riya reached out a hand to stroke her arm.

"Starting now," Courtney said, taking several steps backward. "Go get breakfast. I'll use the time you bought me with whatever lie you told to take a nice, long, hot-water-stealing shower."

Riya continued heading the way they'd been walking, but she turned around and walked backward. "Did you just intentionally make me think about you taking a long, hot shower?"

The thought hadn't even occurred to her, but now she was thinking about Riya thinking about her in the shower and her skin prickled. Courtney coquetted, bringing her shoulder up to meet her chin, then finishing with an over-the-top wink.

Riya tripped, stumbling before she caught herself and

stopped. "You'll be the death of me yet, Courtney Chastain."

Courtney laughed, resisting the urge to race to her and wrap her in her arms. "That's the plan." She had the feeling that flirting with Riya could become her new addiction. It was fun and — bizarrely — genuine. Honest. Courtney had cultivated the reputation of an incurable flirt, but she couldn't remember if she'd ever meant it the same way she did with Riya.

Riya shook her head and turned to walk away normally. "I'll get you a banana and a box of Frosted Flakes," she tossed over her shoulder like it meant so little.

But the fact that, even three years later, Riya remembered her favorite breakfast from when they'd been children, that meant a whole lot more than Courtney would ever admit.

Courtney allowed herself several seconds to watch Riya walk away, openly enjoying the way her hips swayed on top of her bronze, toned legs. She craved their next minute alone together, knowing the wait would be a sweet torture.

Chapter Ten

Dee dropped a full plate in front of Riya before her butt had even hit the bench. "Saved you some."

"You're the best," Riya said in way of thanks. She picked up a spoon and scooped a giant heap of buttered grits into her mouth.

The announcements had finished, and Riya had about four minutes to eat before they cleared the cafeteria to set up for the next activity. Remembering her promise to Courtney, she swiped a banana from the tray and popped up to grab a box of the cereal they always kept on hand for the picky breakfast eaters. When she turned to head back to her seat, a T-shirted man chest stopped her. She craned her neck to see Colt Chastain standing in her way. His blond hair stuck up at all angles.

"Do you know where my sister is?" he asked.

Oh my God, does he know? How? Who told him? How much does he suspect? How pissed is Courtney going to be? All of those thoughts passed through her mind in less than a nanosecond.

"You share a bunk with her, right?" he asked. "You must have seen her."

Her overactive mind hit the brakes. "Yeah, I saw her."

"Is everything okay? She didn't practice this morning, and she never misses breakfast."

Riya nodded, unsure how much of the truth to share. "She'll be at the first session."

"Was it the vodka?" Colt continued without giving Riya a chance to answer. "I knew I should've stopped her. She never drinks."

"She doesn't?" In the past two days, Riya'd overheard Courtney tell Bridget how much she'd drank at this or that party several times.

Something in Riya's tone caught Colt's attention. He scrutinized her expression. "She's two different people," he said. "The real one, and the one she thinks everybody expects her to be. Though, I guess you know that better than most, don't you?"

Riya inhaled sharply and choked on her own spit. Through the coughs, she spat out, "Me?" He knew something, he must. "I don't know anything."

"Yeah, you know the real her," he said. "From when we were kids." The skin between his eyebrows wrinkled. "You're weird this morning."

Riya shrugged, thinking up an excuse. "I'm tired, not quite awake yet."

He nodded like that made perfect sense. "How late were you up with Courtney, anyway?"

Riya couldn't figure out if he was testing her or she was just being hypersensitive. Either he suspected something and was fishing for information or he knew everything and was testing Riya's loyalty on Courtney's behalf. Or she was overreacting entirely.

"Derek told me he left her with you last night and that

she'd been really drunk," Colt added. "How bad was it?"

"Pretty bad," Riya said. "I held her hair. I think she threw up everything she's ever eaten."

He probably didn't need to know that, but Courtney's drunkenness felt like a much safer topic than anything else they could talk about.

Colt grimaced. "Sorry."

Riya felt compelled to say more, to keep talking. "I gave her water and medicine this morning. It's going to be a rough day for her."

"She doesn't deserve you." There was something in his tone that made Riya nervous.

Her gaze jerked to his eyes, and he waited. Of course Courtney deserved her. More, even. Courtney was amazing. She deserved anything and everything. Riya, remembering the panicked look in Courtney's eyes that morning, clamped her mouth shut until she could come up with a normal non-romantic thing to say.

"I gave her some ibuprofen." She tried to sound dismissive. "It's nothing anyone else wouldn't do."

Colt twisted his lips together. "Riiiiight." He drew out the word.

Dee materialized next to her. "You going hiking again, Riya?" And then, as if he hadn't been the main reason she'd come over instead of waiting to ask Riya on the walk back to their cabin, she said. "Oh, hey, Colt."

Colt grinned down at her. Not a polite smile or a casual good-morning smile, but a full-on "I'm so happy to see you" smile.

"Good morning, Lola," he said with a deep smirk.

Dee giggled, rolling her eyes playfully. Well. Riya had missed something, it seemed.

"I told you not to call me that," Dee said, but zero conviction backed up her words.

"I had my schedule changed so I can go hiking with y'all. Is that okay?" Colt asked without taking his eyes from Dee.

"Of course," Riya said before mumbling something about having to go and backing away as discreetly as she could manage.

She caught up with the twins and Elise as they cleared the table. She scooped her apple and Courtney's banana from her plate before Tiffany piled it on top of her own.

"So…" Riya trailed off, indicating Dee and Colt with a twitch of her head.

"Yep," Stefanie and Tiffany said in unison. It was kinda freaky when they did that.

Elise flashed a huge, toothy smile, and those two words were all that was needed to settle the Dee and Colt conversation.

The four of them waited for a minute outside the door, but Dee didn't appear, so they headed back to the cabin to get ready for the day.

Courtney was nowhere to be found, but her bed was made and all her things had been put away. After dropping the banana and cereal on Courtney's bed, Riya went to the bathroom partly just to see if Courtney was in there. She washed her face, used the toilet, and washed her hands before returning to her bunk.

Dee came jogging through the front door, beaming.

Tiffany threw the shirt she'd just been about to put on at Dee. "Look who decided to show up," she said, teasing.

Laughing, Dee tossed it back at her. "Put your clothes on."

Riya suffered a flash of jealousy. Though she understood Courtney's need for time, she hated that she couldn't celebrate their budding relationship with her friends.

She opened the drawer with her T-shirts and reached her hand in. But it was empty. Confused, she opened another drawer. Nothing. Only then did she notice that her toiletry bag, which had been sitting on top of the dresser, was also gone. She searched around and realized the blanket, pillow, and sheet no longer lay on her bed. She'd been so focused on Courtney's bed when she came in that she hadn't even noticed.

"Guys," she said, interrupting her friends' joking around. "All my stuff is gone."

Four smiles fell from four faces as they turned their attention to her. She pointed to her empty drawers and the empty spot under their bunk where her bag had been.

"They're kicking you out," Stefanie said.

Riya's stomach turned to stone. *No. Not now.* Not after Courtney had finally opened up to her.

"What did you do?" Tiffany asked.

Riya racked her brain, trying to think. She'd stayed out way past curfew with Courtney, but Courtney's stuff was all still there, so it couldn't be that. Could it? Unless her parents, bigshot lawyers, had somehow argued for her to stay.

Elise was the first to crack. It sounded like a cough, at first. She covered her mouth as a strange mewling escaped her lips. Dee turned away before an unmistakable laugh burst from her mouth. Finally, the twins joined in and everyone laughed openly. Riya scowled at her friends before smiling, relieved.

"Sorry, that was mean," Stefanie said.

"So I'm not getting kicked out?" Riya said. "Where's my stuff, then?"

"It's an old camp prank," Tiffany added.

Something twisted in Riya's stomach. Courtney had pranked her? After the kisses and the confessions, Riya had assumed a cease fire at the very least.

Dee took in Riya's outfit—a plain white tee on top of a white sports bra and black volleyball shorts—and tossed her a blue sports bra from her dresser. "You're going to need this."

Riya caught the sports bra and stared at it, still confused. "I don't get it. Where's my stuff?"

"Put that on. One sec," Dee said. She changed in record time, slipping on tennis shoes without tying them.

Riya turned toward her bunk and changed into Dee's sports bra, unsure why it was necessary.

"You're probably going to miss hiking." She sounded apologetic as she led Riya outside.

Halfway to the office side of the lake, the twins and Elise caught up, running until they fell into step with Riya. Tiffany French-braided her hair as she walked. If Riya still wasn't so confused about where her stuff was, she would've asked Tiffany how she managed it. Riya could braid her hair and she could walk, but doing both at the same time would result in disaster, she was sure.

Dee marched straight onto the beach and extended an arm, pointing at a dark shape about a third of the way across the lake. It looked to be a kayak with a dark lump in the seat.

Riya stared at it, then turned to Dee, who nodded.

"My stuff is out there?" She squinted at the lump. She supposed that could be her bag.

"Yep," Tiffany said.

"Courtney pulled out an old favorite for this one," Stefanie added.

Riya glanced down at her borrowed sports bra. "So why do I need this?"

Dee blushed a little. "I didn't think you'd want to come out of the water wearing a white sports bra." She raised her eyebrows at Riya, asking if she needed to explain further.

That was thoughtful, but she still didn't see why it was necessary. "I can just take another one of the kayaks out to get it, though."

Elise stepped forward, toeing the water. "All the others are chained and locked if it's not designated lake time," she said. "They leave one unlocked in case of an emergency."

Did everyone know the full playbook on this prank except for her? Volleyball camps never took place on lakes, so she was not familiar with this particular flavor of "hide someone's stuff."

"So I have to swim out to get it." She grew grateful for the borrowed sports bra.

Her friends nodded. She couldn't believe Courtney had done this to her after last night. It made Riya realize how serious she'd been about continuing on, business as usual. That she'd go to all this trouble, as terrible as she felt, to make everyone think nothing had changed made Riya's stomach sink.

"And make sure you don't tip over the kayak on your way back," Elise added, making a face. "Hypothetically. For example." Nothing about that sounded hypothetical.

Stefanie elbowed her. "I told you I'd go out and get it for you."

Elise smiled at her friend. "Some things you just gotta do for yourself."

"It's farther than it looks," Tiffany offered. "Pace yourself."

Dee glanced over her shoulder. Campers walked by in a steady stream, on their way to the first activity of the day. The hiking group would depart from the bonfire field in just a couple of minutes.

"Go," Riya said to Dee. "Thanks for the…you know." She motioned at her chest area.

"Are you sure? I feel bad leaving you," Dee said.

"You told Colt you'd be there," Riya said, putting more cheer into her voice than she felt. "He'll be heartbroken if you stand him up."

Dee cast one more glance at the kayak floating on the lake, then at Riya. "Thank you. And good luck." She took off toward the bonfire area, walking on the boy's side of the lake.

Riya turned to the other three. "You guys don't have to stay and watch me. Go do whatever you were planning on doing."

Elise glanced at Stefanie and gave Riya a sympathetic look. "We were going to make a dreamcatcher," she said. "I was looking forward to it."

"Please, go." Riya shooed her hands at them. "I'll be fine." The two walked away with their thanks and apologies.

Tiffany plopped on the sand, sitting on her heels.

"What are you doing?" Riya asked.

"Dane's not on duty yet," Tiffany said. "He won't be here for at least an hour. There aren't any water sports planned until the second session."

Dane was one of the lifeguards, Riya remembered from the first night.

"I'm a great swimmer," Riya insisted. She didn't want anyone to lose out on anything fun because of Courtney.

"Tate Ramsden drowned to death," Tiffany said with no further explanation. Tiffany was a woman of few words. She was stoic. Riya liked that. Usually, anyway.

"Who is Tate Ramsden?"

"He was a competitive swimmer at Dartmouth who died last year at a YMCA," Tiffany said. "So I'll be right here until you're safely back on shore."

The thing about people who didn't say much was no one could argue with the few things they did choose to say.

Not wasting any time, Riya waded into the water and dove toward the center of the lake. As she sliced her arms through the calm surface in even strokes, doubts crept in to her thoughts. Courtney wanted to act like nothing had changed so much that she hauled all of Riya's belongings to the middle of the lake while suffering one hell of a hangover. Riya couldn't help wondering if, for Courtney, it was more than an act. If she'd regretted her drunken declarations and wanted to take them back. Or...maybe...the drunken declarations themselves had been part of a larger act. Courtney couldn't be so cruel as to play that kind of prank on Riya.

Could she?

• • •

Courtney went to archery that morning because she knew Bridget would be there. She did not know David would also be there. And Derek. Crap.

Bridget only ever annoyed Courtney when she flirted. The girl subscribed to the belief that guys only liked stupid girls who never challenged them, so her giggles and inane agreements throughout the entire session had Courtney feeling nauseated all over again. Bridget, despite her inclination to act dumb and preference of talking about shallow things, was incredibly smart. Courtney considered willful ignorance a terrible waste. This morning, especially, it kept reminding Courtney of her own grand lie. No one could fully be who they were. Except Riya, who was so fiercely herself. Riya knew exactly who she was and lived her life without apologizing for it.

Derek kept trying to make polite conversation, showing he harbored no hard feelings, which was sweet of him. Courtney wasn't in the mood, though.

Their instructor that day was one of the male counselors, so she told him she had "lady trouble" and he rapidly excused her to leave twenty minutes before the session ended. On her walk back to the cabin, she spotted dark clouds on the north horizon. She hoped they'd blow west instead of dumping rain on Pine Ridge.

She walked straight to her cabin and dropped into her bed, tossing an arm over her eyes. She'd never allowed alcohol to do this to her before. After experiencing a hangover, she wondered why anyone did. Though David had drank twice what she did and seemed totally fine today, so maybe some took it better than others.

Her eyelids drifted closed just as the doorknob rattled. Courtney startled awake. Framed by a rectangle of painful sunlight, a delightfully curvy frame Courtney knew well stood in the doorway. Before the door opened all the way, Courtney stood on her feet. Riya held a bundle over her shoulder like it was Santa's bag. Her firm stomach was bare, and the blue sports bra and shorts she wore clung to her skin like saran wrap.

She looked like a dream.

"Riya." Courtney rushed forward and grabbed Riya's free hand.

Riya shook it roughly, throwing Courtney's hand off. The gesture stung.

"Are you mad?" Courtney asked. "About the—"

Riya's eyes slid sideways, fast. Another figure entered the doorway. Stefanie. Or Tiffany. Courtney could never tell which was which. She carried Riya's duffel. Courtney backed away from the towering twin, who glared at her.

"What are you doing here?" the twin asked, moving to stand between Courtney and Riya.

Her hostility switched on Courtney's defensive systems. "I don't have to explain myself to you. What are *you* doing here?"

Riya grabbed for her bag in the twin's hand. "Tiffany, it's fine." Riya tugged on the handle, turning the girl toward her. "Thank you so much for helping me."

Courtney watched Riya's fingers brush Tiffany's hand and her temper flared. Then she noticed Riya's sports bra again. It was navy now that it was soaked, but probably royal blue dry. And Riya had definitely been wearing a white sports bra that morning. A blue one would have stood out underneath her thin white cotton shirt. Courtney'd even thought about it as she shoved the kayak out into the water. She remembered being grateful everyone would be busy at activities when Riya climbed out of the water—and regretful she would also miss it. But Tiffany had been there.

"Where'd you get that?" Courtney asked, pointing at the mystery garment.

Riya turned on her heel and followed Courtney's outstretched finger. She frowned. "Dee gave it to me so I wouldn't have to walk around here with my nipples visible for everyone to see. You know, because she cares about my feelings." She marched over and heaved the bundle of bedding onto her bed before dropping her duffel to the floor and kicking it under Courtney's bed.

Oh, shit. Riya *was* mad.

She unraveled the bundle and started making her bed. Tiffany walked to the bathroom, throwing daggers over her shoulder at Courtney, warning her.

As soon as she heard the click of the bathroom stall door being locked, Courtney rushed to Riya, slipping her arms around her stomach. "Please don't be mad," she murmured into the back of Riya's neck, her lips brushing Riya's warm skin as they moved.

Cold wetness seeped from Riya's bra through Courtney's shirt, and her damp shorts pressed directly against Courtney's thigh. A single chill rocketed down Courtney's spine. Riya spun in place, sliding the warm skin of her stomach against the insides of Courtney's arms. When she faced Courtney, her expression was drawn tight in anger, but she softened almost immediately. When they stood like this, Riya's chest fit nicely just below Courtney's much smaller breasts.

They fit together so perfectly.

"Why did you do this?" Riya whispered. She slipped her arms around Courtney so her forearms hung on her hips.

"We're supposed to act normal, remember?" Courtney

said.

Riya shook her head, closing her eyes. "None of this is normal."

Courtney tilted her head down and kissed her left eyelid. Riya leaned into her lips and made a small, happy sound that shot a thrill through Courtney's torso. Courtney kissed the indentation to the side of her eye, her left temple, the hollow of her cheek. Given enough time, she'd kiss every inch of Riya's skin. Riya's eyes fluttered open and focused on Courtney's. They were a deep, rich brown flecked with golden sparks. Riya tilted her chin up and pulled Courtney's hips into hers.

Courtney's pulse pounded through every part of her. While every single cell of Courtney's body told her how right this felt and how perfect they were for each other, an encoded part of her brain kept trying to tell her it was wrong. A mistake. But how could anything that made her entire body hum with bliss be anything but absolute truth? Truth, with a capital *T*.

She pressed her hands against Riya's back, compelling her closer still. Riya's lips parted, and Courtney stood entranced by their pillowy softness, by the soft brush of breath on the skin of her neck.

The toilet flushed. Courtney and Riya jumped apart.

Riya sighed and turned back to the task of making her bed. Courtney took a few steps away, unsure what to do with her gaze or her hands. Water ran in the sink for a couple of seconds before Tiffany turned it off and came back into the room.

Tiffany spoke directly to Riya, like Courtney didn't even exist. Probably a good thing, since Courtney had still failed to pull herself together. Her chest rose and fell too fast. Sweat dampened her armpits, so she clenched her arms tight to her sides.

"Stefanie and Elise are checking out the campfire cooking thing after lunch," Tiffany said. "You going to that?"

"Sure." Riya's voice came out husky, which sent a jolt of satisfaction through Courtney.

"You should get out of those wet clothes before we have to leave for lunch," Tiffany suggested. Her tone held absolutely no flirtation in it, but Courtney vowed to watch her closely from here on out.

"Right," Riya mumbled, distracted. She bent over to pull a change of clothes out of her bag. Riya's already short shorts slid up another half an inch, and Courtney's desire flared like a fire engulfing a barrel of oil. Riya turned toward her bed and struggled to pull the wet sports bra over her head. The skin of her back was smooth, and the gentle curves of her shoulder blades gleamed like silk. Courtney's mouth went dry. She found something else to stare at before Riya could shimmy out of the shorts.

Courtney found herself fantasizing about what might have happened if Riya'd come back without her bodyguard. Suddenly, she realized both Tiffany and a fully clothed Riya stared at her expectantly.

"Huh?" Courtney said.

"We were wondering if you would deign to make an appearance at lunch?" Tiffany asked.

Courtney narrowed her eyes at the girl's mocking tone.

"It's your turn to get the food," Riya clarified, the words rushing from her lips as she looked anywhere but at Courtney.

Courtney nodded and gestured to the door, indicating they should all head over. The atmosphere among the three on the walk to the cafeteria was thick and palpable. The gray clouds on the horizon that morning had drifted closer and now hovered on the edge of the camp's borders.

Once they'd passed the youngest girls' cabins, Colt jogged up to Courtney, calling her name and grinning like an idiot. "I've got great news," he called.

A couple feet from them, he stopped, catching sight of

Riya. "Hey, we missed you on the hike. Dee said something came up."

"Maybe tomorrow," Riya said before sidestepping him and rushing to the cafeteria. Tiffany followed.

"What was that all about?" Colt asked.

Courtney wondered why Delores hadn't told him the truth. She'd known Riya liked Courtney and thought Courtney returned her feelings. If she suspected something was going on, Courtney doubted she'd keep their secret from Colt.

"You have good news?" she reminded him, changing the subject.

He watched her for a couple more seconds, evaluating her every facial twitch. Courtney pulled on a practiced mask and focused on keeping her body relaxed.

"David's dad is coming in for the talent show," he announced, imbuing the words with great significance.

Courtney waited for further explanation, but none came.

"That's good for him?" she said, confused. A lot of parents came a couple of hours early to check out the end-of-session talent show. Hers never did, but they were busy and couldn't make the trip. "I didn't realize David was going to perform."

Not getting the reaction he expected, Colt shook his hands in frustration. "You're so self-absorbed."

Only her twin could say something like that to her and get away with it unscathed.

"Rude." She started walking toward the cafeteria. "Are you going to get to the point?"

"David's dad is the Board President of the Riverdrake Foundation."

With those last two words, her always graceful walk turned into a barely contained stumble. She hadn't heard him correctly, no way. "That's the one that gives scholarships for students pursuing degrees in the arts?" She needed confirmation.

Colt nodded, a smug grin stretching across his face. "Full scholarships. Completely merit-based."

A cold sweat broke across her forehead, and her feet refused to take another step. "Shit."

Colt raised a hand to her elbow to steady her. "The good kind of shit, though, right?"

Courtney laughed. "Yeah." This could be her chance. She barely dared to hope for it. If she got a Riverdrake scholarship, she truly wouldn't need her parents' money to go to Juilliard—if she even got in, that was.

Too many ifs, but just enough maybes to give her a glimmer of hope.

"We have to pick a song." Words spilled out of her in an agitated cadence. "I have to start choreographing it today. Only, like, two weeks. Not enough time, no time."

Firm hands gripped her shoulders, shaking her just enough to grab her attention. "Court. Chill. You got this."

She drew in a deep breath, then blew it out, puffing her cheeks. "I can do this."

In a way, the talent show in this mountain summer camp was now more important than her Juilliard audition, though they both depended on each other. And she should probably be a little nicer to David than she'd been this morning. It couldn't hurt.

"I have an idea about the song, actually," Colt said, running a hand through his hair. "You remember Sergei Polunin's dance to 'Take Me to Church,' right?"

Courtney nodded. "But I can't do that, everyone's seen that video. I can't be derivative."

Colt shook his head. "No. I mean, something similar. An edgy dance to a pop song. I've been working on a piano cover of Adele's 'Hello.'"

Most of her performances over the past five years had

been to Colt's piano playing, or an orchestra playing for her dance company. The last time she'd competed to a recorded song, she'd choked miserably. She swore it was a curse. Colt argued that he had spoiled her. Either way, she refused to perform to anything other than live music anymore. Practice was okay, but the energy of live music transformed a dance to something great.

Closing her eyes, Courtney played the song in her head, rocking to the rhythm. Almost immediately, a vision took shape in her mind's eye. It was a beautiful song and deserved an exquisite dance. Ever so slowly, the corners of her mouth turned up, and a smile inched across her face.

Colt pumped a fist in the air. "I knew you'd love it."

Chapter Eleven

The next day at lunch, Riya took apart her BLT, tossing everything but the bacon to the far side of her tray. Her appetite was nonexistent, but she never turned away bacon. Riya had been quieter than usual at lunch, poking at tomato seeds with her pinkie finger. She obsessed over the way Courtney turned hot and cold, wondering how she could be so convincing as she pretended to dislike Riya. When others were around, her disdain was so believable, Riya had a hard time convincing herself what had happened on the dock and yesterday while Tiffany'd been in the bathroom was real. For the thousandth time, she puzzled over which version of Courtney was the act.

Riya felt the separation like a knife twisting in her stomach. On their walk that morning, they'd talked, but they hadn't touched. Courtney'd grown so paranoid of anyone seeing them together that Riya felt like they'd spent less time together than before they'd kissed.

Unlike Courtney, Riya wore her emotions like a manifestation. She couldn't hide them. The harder she tried, the more obvious they were.

Her friends, understandably, had assumed she was upset about Courtney's prank. Which, when she thought about it, only sent Riya further into despondency. She wished she could tell her friends what was going on with her. She wanted their advice, their understanding, and—she could admit it—their sympathy.

Riya, Dee, and Tiffany ducked out of lunch half an hour early. It was time, Tiffany had declared, for payback.

"I have a special treat I prepared especially for Courtney," Dee had said, tenting her fingers in a mockery of villainy. "It would be an honor to prank her on your behalf."

Knowing Courtney expected her to keep up the prank war, but lacking the motivation, Riya was happy to let her friends take over. She cared so little, she didn't even ask Dee what the prank was. Back at their cabin, Dee pulled from her bag a skewer and a tube of the gel that numbed your mouth when your tooth ached.

"Where's her bathroom kit?" Dee asked, waggling the tube in her hand.

Riya showed her the sturdy canvas bag on top of Courtney's dresser, and Dee poked around the bag before pulling out Courtney's toothpaste. Extreme whitening. Wintergreen flavor. Riya looked between the two tubes, realizing what Dee had planned. She had to admit, it was clever.

Dee flipped open the top and scooped out some of the toothpaste with the skewer. Tiffany snickered when Dee handed her the toothpaste-coated skewer. Dee squeezed the smaller tube of the numbing gel into the space she'd vacated and flipped the top shut with a satisfied smirk.

"I can't wait until tonight," Tiffany said as she helped Dee return the toothpaste to its original location.

Dee held up one hand to each of her friends. Tiffany

slapped it with gusto. Riya acquiesced, smacking her palm against Dee's.

Volleyball for the older campers was every other day. Alternating days hosted baseball, which was what they'd played yesterday. Catching had never been one of Riya's skills. She told Dee it wasn't her fault she'd trained in two sports where catching the ball was literally punished with running laps. Throwing was easy; it was fundamentally the same as a serve. But she didn't even want to start thinking about batting.

At one point yesterday, Dee was laughing so hard she had to call a timeout.

"It's not that funny," Riya had said, growing increasingly self-conscious.

"I'm sorry," Dee choked out in between fits of laughter. "It's just, you're so good at volleyball, I thought you'd have some kind of natural talent."

Riya shook her head. "I wasn't good at volley when I started, either. I have zero natural athletic ability. I'm just stubborn and practice obsessively."

Luckily, it started raining, and they had to quit playing half an hour early. It had been cloudy and raining off and on for two days now.

She was looking forward to a sport she could play better than a toddler. At that point, she'd take soccer or even basketball. Anything. But today was a volleyball day and that gave her something to be happy about. Or so she thought until she strolled up to the court to find Colt, Derek, David, and Bridget already there. No Courtney. Bridget had claimed the spot Elise had sat in the other day with a pink and red striped towel, but the tall blonde was nowhere to be seen. Elise, the twins, and Dee arrived a minute after Riya.

Riya spent the entire warm-up time debating whether to ask Colt where Courtney was. She practiced it in her head, attempting to sound nonchalant, as though she didn't care about the answer. But she did. And she cared about the answer to the question she couldn't ask: *Why is she avoiding me?*

When Colt called her name, her heart leapt into her throat. She panicked, worried she'd voiced her thoughts aloud. His bare feet flopped through the sand toward her.

"Hey," he said, smiling. "Why haven't you been coming to singing?"

"Oh." The panic abandoned her, leaving her feeling empty. She hadn't yet told Colt her decision. "I appreciate you offering to play for me, but I don't think I'm going to do the talent show." After the one class, where she'd nearly had a heart attack trying to sing in front of a couple of campers, she knew there was no way she'd be able to sing in front of the entire camp. Just thinking about it now made her skin itch.

He stuffed his hands in the pockets of his swimming trunks and considered her. "Okay, I get it."

Riya relaxed. Of course Colt would understand. He always understood. More than he let on, she thought. Then, he said the only thing that could possibly change her mind.

"Courtney will be disappointed."

Riya's mind went blank. "What? She will? Did she say something?"

Colt laughed. "Yeah, that you didn't have a chance against her and you should just quit before she embarrasses you."

Riya's mouth dropped open, but before she could agonize over exactly what that meant, he clarified.

"Which means she's worried about you beating her."

Riya, beating Courtney in a talent competition? The idea was so absurd, a laugh burst from Riya's lips. "So wouldn't she be happy about me dropping out?"

He shook his head. "Court's a competitor, through and through. Knowing someone else might beat her, especially now, will make her better."

Riya got that. Her team always played better against a great team than one they knew they could easily beat. "What do you mean, especially now?"

Colt told her about the Riverdrake scholarship and David's dad.

"That's good," Riya said because it was what she was supposed to say, but her words fell flat. Courtney, of all people, did not need a scholarship. It didn't make any sense.

Colt raised his eyebrow and waited.

"Why does she care about a scholarship?" Riya asked.

He cocked his head, creasing his brow. "She didn't tell you?"

Riya shook her head.

Becky blew the whistle for the game to begin. They played three games before Colt and Riya could speak again. Tiffany and Stefanie always played on opposite teams, but they switched up the teams every round. The twins were too dominant to play on the same team no matter who played against them.

The longer she thought about the scholarship, the less sense it made. Courtney wasn't the type of person to accept a scholarship just because she could, taking away an opportunity from someone else. Or, at least, she hadn't been four years ago.

During a water break, Riya asked Colt the question again.

Colt seemed uncomfortable. "I probably shouldn't say."

"Oh. Okay," Riya said, her mind spinning with possibilities. Was their family having money problems?

When they returned to the court, she threw herself into the game. Afterward, she was chugging what was left in her water bottle when Colt approached her again.

"So what are you thinking about singing?" he asked. "For the talent show?"

Riya sighed. "I told you, I don't want to do it."

Colt's eyes scrunched. "Oh. I thought you'd want to help Courtney."

"Help her?" She'd do anything to help Courtney, but she didn't see how this qualified.

"By giving her someone to compete against," he clarified.

"So she can maybe get a scholarship she doesn't need?" She shook her head. "You know how nervous I get singing in front of other people."

Colt forced a slow breath out between his lips, puffing out his cheeks. "Our parents don't want her to study dance," he blurted. "She has a shot at Juilliard but they told her they won't pay for it."

"Whoa." Juilliard. That was huge. Even artless Riya knew that. But why hadn't Courtney told her any of this? Life-changing things were happening and Courtney hadn't mentioned any of it.

"She's spent every minute she can dancing. She's done nothing but obsess since she found out about it yesterday."

Yesterday. Riya guessed that's why she hadn't seen much of Courtney in the past day.

"Every minute, huh?" Riya eyed the arts and crafts hut on the other side of the tennis courts. "Hey, I gotta go."

She waved at Colt as she took off.

"Don't tell her I told you, okay?" Colt called after her.

She tossed him a thumbs up over her shoulder.

. . .

Courtney opened the door of the arts hut with her left hand, pulling up the Adele song on her phone with her right. She had a solid thirty minutes before dinner. The door fell shut behind her with a crack of wood on wood. She dropped her water bottle on the first table inside the door.

"Hey, Court."

Courtney started and almost dropped her phone. Riya stood no more than four feet away from her. She wore a bright yellow sporty two-piece swimsuit, sturdy enough to survive volleyball but still sexy as any bikini. Courtney felt a deep, sudden affection for the warm weather that allowed Riya to walk around in that outfit. Sun flooded the room, highlighting her caramel skin and setting her dark hair shimmering.

Courtney'd been so focused on choreographing her dance, she hadn't seen Riya except at meals and bedtime. Truth be told, Courtney had been avoiding her at activities and meals. Pretending she didn't care for her was so much harder than she'd thought. She'd catch Riya's gaze across a room, and it'd be all she could do not to run to her. When boys flirted with her, Courtney wanted to put her arm around Riya, claiming her in front of everyone. *Mine.*

Riya smiled. Wisps of hair framed her face, and they swayed as she moved. Lord, she was so exceptionally beautiful.

"I don't want to interrupt." Riya watched her through thick black lashes. "But I wanted to see you."

Slowly, oh so slowly, Riya stepped closer. She reached up and pushed a stray strand of hair behind Courtney's ear, her fingertips trailing along Courtney's cheek. Her touch left a trail of fire on Courtney's skin. Courtney raised her arm to take Riya's hand in her own.

They crashed into each other. A full day and night's worth of pent-up emotion washed over her. She kissed Riya like a drowning man gulped air, backing her up until Riya's shoulders were against the wood plank wall.

Courtney pressed her palms into Riya's stomach, spreading her fingers over the skin. She marveled at the combination of strength and softness there.

Riya tore her mouth away to trail kisses from Courtney's jawbone down her neck. Every press of her lips against Courtney's skin sent pulses of pleasure through Courtney's entire body. How had she survived an entire day without this? How had she survived seventeen years without this?

Not trusting her legs to support her much longer, Courtney sat in one of the plastic chairs, pulling Riya down to sit on her lap. Riya placed both hands on the sides of Courtney's face. She smelled of sunscreen and sweat with traces of baby powder.

"I've missed you," Riya breathed.

"I'm sorry," Courtney said, punctuating her statement with a kiss to the spot just below Riya's ear. "I've missed you, too."

"Really?" Riya's voice cracked.

"So, so much." How could she doubt it? Every second Courtney wasn't dancing she spent thinking about Riya. She daydreamed scenarios about them getting lost in the woods together and finding a hidden cave, about kissing her until Riya's mouth was red and Courtney couldn't feel her lips anymore.

A smile flickered across Riya's lips before she pressed them again to Courtney's.

Behind her, the door smacked shut. Riya froze, her head jerking up to face the sound. Courtney's heart stopped.

"Oh," Colt said. "Sorry Riy— Courtney?"

Riya scrambled to her feet, and Courtney spun to face her brother, her heart pounding painfully against her ribs. All three of them stood in stunned silence for several seconds.

A grin shattered Colt's shocked expression. He laughed, clapping his hands with glee.

"You're not upset?" Courtney asked.

His eyes volleyed back and forth between the two girls. "Well, honestly, I am."

Courtney stiffened.

"I'm a little mad you didn't tell me about this, but I'm so happy for you that I'm going to let it slide."

Courtney watched her brother closely as he gave Riya a tiny fist-pump. Riya laughed and dropped her gaze to her feet.

Her brother was…really happy. For her. After catching her making out with a girl. Of course, he'd always *said* he'd support her no matter what, but for him to actually see it and react this way… Apparently, Courtney had never given her brother enough credit.

Riya stepped closer to her, slipping her hand into Courtney's. Courtney turned to look at her, and Riya gave her hand a squeeze.

"You okay?" Riya whispered.

Courtney nodded. She felt relieved. Courtney'd never hidden anything from her brother. He was her best friend, always her ally. Now he knew her closest-held secret, her truth. And he accepted it all. So easily.

Colt grew awkward, glancing at the door. "Um, should I go or…?"

"No," Riya said. "It's okay."

Courtney nodded in agreement. He'd already killed the mood, anyway. And touching Riya in front of someone else sent a special kind of thrill through her. Someone else knowing made it feel more real, less like a recurring dream.

"Good," Colt said, pulling up a chair. "Because I have questions."

"Oh Lord," Courtney said.

"How long?" Colt asked.

"Four years," Riya said at the exact same time Courtney said, "Two days."

They looked at each other. Pink swept across Riya's cheeks and she shrugged. Riya had been sure for so long, and she'd waited all that time for Courtney to realize it.

"How come no one told me?"

Courtney didn't have an answer for that. It seemed unfair to say she thought her brother might disapprove, but she'd been scared.

"We're not telling anyone," Riya said, sliding her gaze sideways, checking for Courtney's confirmation.

Colt watched Riya closely. "Why not?"

Riya did not waver. "Courtney's not ready to come out yet and I respect that."

A surge of affection filled Courtney's chest. She lifted Riya's hand to her lips and planted a soft kiss on her knuckles.

Colt nodded, but his mouth twisted. Courtney knew that look. She checked the clock on the wall.

"You should head over and get changed before dinner," Courtney told Riya, motioning to the bathing suit she still wore. "Colt and I will follow in a couple of minutes."

Sorrow twisted Riya's features. Courtney squeezed her hand and kissed Riya's temple. It was a promise, one she knew Riya would understand.

On her way out the door, Colt offered her his fist. Laughing and shaking her head, she raised her own and mashed their knuckles together.

Seconds after the door clanked shut, Colt stared intensely into Courtney's eyes.

"What?" she challenged.

"You know what," he said.

"I thought you were happy for me?" She stood stock still, returning his stare.

Colt, as always, ignored her attempt to derail. "Don't hurt her."

"I don't want to," Courtney said, but preemptory guilt twisted painfully in her stomach. In a couple of weeks, they'd all have to go home. There was no way she and Riya could have a happy ending. But there was no reason why they couldn't have a happy summer. That would have to be enough. A few perfect weeks by the lake would have to carry her through whatever else waited in her future.

Before she knew it, the taste of salt filled her mouth and her vision blurred. Colt was up and hugging her before she even realized she was crying.

"What am I going to do?" She choked on her words.

Colt hushed and rocked her until her sobs subsided. Then he pulled back, examining her face. "You really want my advice?"

She nodded, wiping tears from her eyes.

"Even though I wish you felt differently, I get if you don't want everyone to know you're in a relationship with Riya."

Courtney began to speak, but he held up a finger. "But pretending like you still hate each other is torturing you both. She's mopey. You're more of a bitch than usual. It's not good for anyone."

Courtney chewed her lip as she considered. "You want us to be friends."

"You're already friends in private. Like friends plus, I guess." He motioned to the chair she'd been sitting in when he'd arrived. "Besides, she's terrible at pretending like nothing's going on."

Courtney laughed, remembering catching Riya staring longingly at her dozens of times over the last couple of days. "True."

"A good friendship is basically like dating without the touching anyway," he reasoned. "I mean, on the outside. Consider it a trial run."

Maybe Colt was right. Trying to act like everything was the same as before wasn't working. And with Colt and Dee getting closer, it would appear totally natural. It was only for a couple of weeks, after all. Then she'd have to go back to her normal, suffocating life. It was reasonable to enjoy herself while she could.

Colt walked over to the door and held it open for her. "Time for dinner."

Slowly, they walked on the boys' side of the lake. Colt had already changed for dinner, and Courtney had planned to go straight from dancing. Halfway to the cafeteria, Courtney had decided to try Colt's suggestion.

"I'm lucky to have you, Colt," she said.

He shrugged. "I know."

"Seriously, thank you."

He smiled at her. "Does she make you happy?"

Riya made her nervous and excited. She thrilled her and calmed her. But most importantly, unlike any boy she'd ever dated, Riya made her *feel*.

"Yes," Courtney said.

"I knew it," he whispered.

They walked the rest of the way in silence. To her surprise, Colt escorted her to her table. He flirted with Dee, but Courtney knew what else he was doing. He was easing her transition just by being there. And she loved him for it.

She slid into the seat next to Riya and bumped her shoulder. "Hey," she murmured.

Riya looked up, eyes wide, mouth parted. For a second, Courtney considered abandoning all the rules and kissing her right then, but the crush of people around her reminded her to control herself. The table went silent as Riya's friends saw what was happening.

Courtney lifted her chin in greeting. "What's up?"

Chapter Twelve

Riya couldn't believe it. Courtney had hung out with her all night, laughing and being nice to her friends throughout dinner and the night's ice cream social on the beach. Even Tiffany tolerated her presence. Mostly.

And when no one was looking, she'd brush her arm against Riya's or tickle her fingers on Riya's knee. Whatever Colt had said to Courtney after she'd left, Riya'd have to thank him for it later.

But every furtive touch left Riya wanting more. When Courtney placed her hand on Riya's shoulder as she laughed, Riya barely fought the urge to close the small distance between them and plant a peck on her pink lips.

Everyone sat on the shore, toes dipping in the water as they licked ice cream from little plastic spoons and watched the sun set over the mountains. Riya felt the warmth radiating from Courtney's long body beside her as the last slice of sun disappeared behind a greenish-gray slope. The moment was so perfectly romantic—or it could've been. Riya saw nothing wrong with slipping her arm over Courtney's shoulder and pulling her closer, but she knew Courtney wouldn't see it the same way.

Courtney would flip if she tried it. But why? They were at summer camp, the place where you could be who you wanted to be without worrying about what people back home would think. Courtney didn't even talk to Bridget outside of camp, so Riya couldn't understand why she was so worried about people here finding out about them.

"Earth to Riya," Courtney said, bumping her shoulder against Riya's.

Riya's head jerked up and she found Courtney staring at her, sporting a grin that set her oceanic eyes ablaze with joy. Riya couldn't hold on to her thoughts for long with Courtney gazing up at her like that. Courtney was happy. That was enough for Riya. For now.

Riya rode the high of Courtney's happiness as they all got ready for bed. All the G7A girls were in the bathroom, brushing their hair, washing their faces, taking showers, gossiping about the boys. Stefanie and Elise teased Dee about Colt.

Then, Tiffany elbowed Riya and pointed two sinks over to where Courtney brushed her teeth. Courtney's face twitched in confusion, then her eyes crossed as she looked down at her toothbrush. Riya gasped. The prank. How had she forgotten?

Courtney spat in the sink repeatedly. She looked over, catching Tiffany and Riya watching her.

"What did you do?" she said.

Dee, Elise, and Stefanie's conversation halted. They burst out laughing. Tiffany fisted a hand against her lips and her shoulders shook from laughter.

Courtney stuck her tongue out three times. She smacked her lips together. "I can't feel my tongue." Her words came out slightly garbled.

By then, every other girl in the cabin watched Courtney.

Most were laughing, but a few appeared concerned.

"Wha d oo do?" Courtney asked again. "Dis is freaing me oud."

Riya saw the panic in Courtney's eyes and couldn't let it continue.

She rushed to her side. "It's just that stuff you put on your tooth to numb a toothache. You'll be okay. Rinse it out."

She rubbed her hand twice up and down Courtney's back. Courtney's eyes went wide.

"Sorry," Riya whispered. "I forgot."

Courtney shoveled water into her mouth with her hand and spit it out, repeating the process.

Dee joined them, stifling further laughter. "Sorry, we did it this morning."

"Before you were nice to us," Elise clarified.

Tiffany shrugged. "She put Riya's stuff on the lake. She deserves it."

Courtney's body stiffened, and Riya took a step back, bracing for her anger. Courtney straightened and turned to face Tiffany. Riya didn't know if those two had a history or if they just had clashing personalities, but they really didn't like each other.

The two stared at each other for a couple seconds. Riya wondered if she should do anything. If they started fighting, who would she support? Was it possible to stay neutral?

Then Courtney laughed.

Riya could've cried from the relief she felt. She examined Courtney's expression but found no animosity there.

"Nie one, Diya," Courtney said, unable to pronounce some of the consonants.

And just like that, the night continued as though nothing had happened. It was a miracle. Riya silently promised to buy Colt something nice.

After lights out, Riya changed into her pajamas and

crawled beneath her blanket with a smile on her face. All around her, girls talked for about an hour before the conversations finally ceased entirely. Content, Riya drifted off to sleep.

She didn't know how long she'd been asleep when she started awake. A weight on the inside of her mattress messed with her balance and the springs underneath her creaked. She blinked.

Courtney knelt beside her on her bed. "I couldn't sleep," she whispered.

Riya glanced around the room to discover everyone else soundly asleep. Already lying on her back, she scooched to one side and raised her arm. Smiling, Courtney slid her phone under Riya's pillow before resting her head on Riya's shoulder.

"My tongue is still numb," Courtney said.

Riya chuckled.

The warmth of Courtney's body melted into Riya's side. Riya wrapped her arm around Courtney's back, resting her hand on the bend in Courtney's waist. Courtney made a soft cooing sound before laying her arm across Riya's stomach.

If Riya hadn't already been half asleep, she didn't think she'd be capable of falling asleep with Courtney Chastain lying next to her like she was. But Courtney's body relaxed and her breathing became deep and regular, lulling Riya back into sleep.

They both woke when Courtney's alarm buzzed underneath the pillow a full seventy-five minutes before everyone else would be waking. Courtney greeted her with a sleepy smile and a small kiss at the corner of her mouth before climbing down the ladder, as quiet and stealthy as a cat.

They got ready for their morning practices in comfortable silence. Well, it was mostly silent, except for when Riya dropped her toothpaste when Courtney handed it back to her and it bounced across the tile floor. Courtney shook her head, stifling a giggle.

On the walk to the court, Courtney drifted close to Riya's side, allowing their arms to touch. The intermittent brush of Courtney's skin against hers made Riya's head feel light and slightly woozy.

Their steps fell slow and lazy, taking their time for once. They talked in low voices, heads bent toward each other, about school and parents.

"My parents just don't understand why I would ever make a decision different from the one they would make," Courtney said. "They literally can't even begin to comprehend it."

Riya shook her head in sympathy. She could only imagine how suffocating that could be. Her parents were amazing, she'd always known it, but Courtney's stories about her parents threw hers into stark contrast. Riya had always believed Courtney had the perfect life, but every time Courtney opened up about her parents, a little bit of paint flaked off that picturesque forgery.

When they reached the volleyball court, Courtney spun in a slow circle, checking their surroundings, before planting a long, lingering kiss on Riya's lips.

• • •

The next ten days continued in the same happy compromise. Courtney and Riya were friends in public, which everyone but Bridget and Tiffany accepted without complaint. But Riya could deal with a couple of snide comments, even when Bridget asked Courtney, "Why are you slumming with those losers?" as they walked to the pool one day.

"They're not losers," Courtney said in a tone that dared Bridget to argue with her.

Riya lived for the stolen moments when they were alone and she could feel Courtney's skin on hers for more than a passing graze, when Courtney kissed her like she had no reservations. They never talked about what would happen after camp. There was an unspoken moratorium on the subject. Riya knew her family was moving within a reasonable driving distance of the Chastain estate, so continuing the relationship was feasible. If Courtney wanted to continue it. And that's why Riya never brought it up: she wasn't sure Courtney was ready for talk of the long-term. She couldn't stand it if the answer turned out to be no.

Riya now expected the late-night weight-shift on her mattress. Some nights, she looked forward to it so much that she couldn't fall asleep until Courtney was there in her arms.

Riya'd all but stopped suggesting to Courtney that they take their relationship public. Every time, Courtney's eyes would go wide with panic, and she'd turn distant for a couple of hours. Though Riya wanted it more than anything, she didn't want to deal with the fallout anymore.

Mostly, they cuddled and slept, but sometimes Courtney would kiss her good night and Riya would kiss her back and neither of them wanted to stop.

"I don't think I can sleep without your arms around me anymore," Courtney whispered in Riya's right ear. Her breath tickled Riya's neck.

Riya tightened her right arm around Courtney and pulled her closer, caressing her shoulder with her other hand. Courtney brushed her lips over Riya's neck, planting feather-light kisses she knew made Riya melt into a puddle. Courtney's hand slipped under Riya's shirt, tracing random shapes on her stomach.

Riya held her breath each time Courtney's hand trailed upward. Courtney raised her head and their eyes met. The corner of her mouth quirked up as she traced her hand exquisitely slowly, testing the limits of where they'd gone before.

When Courtney's fingertips skimmed the bottommost curve of Riya's breast, Riya pulled both lips into her mouth and bit down to keep her moan from escaping. Courtney's touch was a live wire, sending bolts of sensation deep into Riya's body.

Courtney's eyes danced with amusement.

Two could play that game.

Riya turned on to her right side to face Courtney. She slipped her free hand to the back of Courtney's neck and pulled her to her, kissing her for all she was worth. Color flashed behind Riya's closed eyelids every time Courtney's tongue moved against hers. When Courtney broke free to catch her breath, Riya's hand followed the line of Courtney's arm down to her hip. She slipped two fingers under the waistband of Courtney's pajama shorts.

Courtney's breath caught.

Riya slid her fingers along the waistband until she reached Courtney's prominent hipbone. Courtney's skin was so impossibly soft and smooth. Lifting the waistband away from Courtney's skin with her middle finger, Riya slowly circled the protrusion with her index finger.

Courtney writhed, then tossed one leg over Riya's thigh. "You are going to drive me insane," she whispered into Riya's shoulder.

"That's the plan." Riya echoed Courtney's own words back to her.

Courtney hooked her leg around Riya's legs and shifted her weight, rolling Riya onto her back with Courtney lying on top. "Not if I drive you crazy first."

Grinning, Riya covered Courtney's mouth with her own.

• • •

Courtney yawned as she worked her way through her regular stretches in the rest time after lunch. Last night with Riya had been incredible, but the late nights were starting to take a toll on her motivation in the mornings. She felt the calendar ticking off the days, and she knew there was only so much time before she'd have to give Riya up and go back to the real world. Every time she thought about it, her chest ached like it was being squeezed in a vise. Courtney wanted to milk the days they had together for as much fun as possible.

Riya sat in the corner, watching. She'd promised to stay hands off so that Courtney could get an hour of solid practice time in. The dance was starting to take shape, but it was still rough and she often forgot what came next.

A distinctive knock sounded at the door. Three quick taps and then a hard knock.

"Yeah," she said.

Colt entered. He'd knocked before entering since that first time he'd walked in on them. He pulled a chair next to Riya and sat down. Courtney hadn't seen him a whole lot in the last week because he'd been spending so much time with Delores—*Dee*, she reminded herself. Her friends called her Dee, and that included Courtney now.

"How is she?" he asked.

"Amazing," Riya said dreamily.

Colt laughed. "I think you might be biased."

He leaned back in the chair, and they both watched in silence as Courtney worked through the song twelve times. When she started her cool down stretches, Colt cleared his throat.

She slowly raised her eyes. "You have something to say?"

"No," he began. "Well, yes, but not about the dance. It's beautiful."

She folded her body at the hips, lengthening her muscles and settling deep into the stretch. "What is it?"

"You should tell Dee," he said.

Courtney snapped to her full height and she glared at her brother. Riya switched her wide-eyed gaze between the two of them.

"Absolutely not," Courtney said.

Riya seemed to shrink back, pressing her back into her chair.

"Court," Colt said, holding up his hands. "Hear me out."

"No. You hear me out. You only found out because you barged in."

Colt stood. "And you thanked me for it, remember?"

"Dee is different," Courtney argued. "I don't trust her."

"I do," Riya spoke up. "She's my best friend here."

Courtney flinched. She'd felt intermittent guilt over not letting Riya tell her friends about them. It was usually a fun part of dating someone—being able to squee at and celebrate with and brag to one's friends as things progressed. But if Dee knew, then it wouldn't be long before her other jock friends knew, and then the whole freaking camp.

Colt threw out an arm to motion to Riya. "See? It would give Riya someone to talk to about the situation, if she needs it."

"She can talk to you. You're her friend," Courtney said. "And why would she need it?"

Colt made a vague gesture like it was obvious. He was getting defensive. Worse, he wasn't trying to convince Courtney it would be to her benefit. Something was up.

"Why?" she asked. "Why do you want me to tell Dee that I'm with Riya?"

He ran a hand through his hair, tugging at the ends. "I don't want to lie to her anymore. She keeps asking me questions. She knows Riya liked you, and she's afraid you're playing with her mind or something."

That hurt. Courtney'd been hanging out with Dee and the

others for almost two weeks. She'd thought they'd become friends.

Riya stood up and walked to Courtney, taking her hands in her own.

"I think we should think about it," Riya said. "It would be nice to have another ally. Another person we don't have to hide from."

Guilt sliced through Courtney. She knew Riya wanted to take their relationship public and only hid it for Courtney. She also knew Riya was used to being out, unembarrassed. Courtney even admired her for it.

"I'm not like you," Courtney said. "I'm not brave."

Courtney'd been thinking about this for a couple of days. While Riya was never confident about how people saw her, she was completely confident in who she was. Courtney was the opposite, but only because Courtney—with her parents' help—had handcrafted the image of who she wanted to be seen as. She played the part so perfectly for so long that she couldn't even recognize herself anymore. Only in the past couple of weeks, when she was alone with Riya or working with Colt on the dance, had she started to discover herself again. Though not many people would understand it, she envied Riya and her quiet confidence.

Riya laughed. "You're one of the bravest people I know. You're risking losing the lifestyle you grew up with so that you can follow your passion."

Panic engulfed her. She never thought of it that way. She secretly harbored the idea that, if she got the scholarship and earned a spot at Juilliard, her parents would see how important it was to her. They'd see how serious she was. They'd support her in achieving her dream. Though, her parents seeing the real her and supporting it was the real dream.

Her hands started to shake. Riya drew her into her arms and rubbed a hand in soothing circles on her back.

Colt fidgeted behind them. "I'm going to go set up for singing class," he said. "Talk it over and let me know. I'm going to have to do some groveling for lying to her for so long if you do decide to tell her." He made a fast escape.

"Do you think it's a good idea to tell Dee?" Courtney asked, clutching Riya against her so she couldn't see her face. She didn't want Riya to see the fear she knew must've been etched into every inch.

"I'd tell everyone if I could," Riya said. "I'd hire someone to write it across the sky."

A confusing combination of affection and panic flooded Courtney's veins with adrenaline. Her entire body tensed, and Riya squeezed her in response.

"Don't worry, I'll wait until you're ready," Riya said. "But you can trust Dee. I trust her."

Courtney loosened her hold on Riya to search her face. Big brown eyes stared back at her, begging her. Riya was wrong. Courtney wasn't brave. But Riya made her brave. Sucking in a deep breath for courage, she nodded. "Okay. We can tell her."

The grin that broke across Riya's face reached to the very depths of Courtney's soul, spreading warmth.

"Thank you, Courtney," she said. "I know how hard this is for you. I'm proud of you."

The last four words filled Courtney to the brim. "The three of us can pull her aside at tonight's bonfire," she said.

Riya waggled her eyebrows. "Then we'll get to watch Colt grovel."

Courtney laughed and glanced at the clock. "We gotta go or we'll be late." She slipped on a tone of nonchalance. "You coming to singing?"

Riya shook her head as they stepped out the door. Courtney asked every other day, and Riya always said no, but she wasn't going to stop asking. She had less than a week to convince Riya to join her and Colt for the talent show. He'd reintroduced his plan for the three of them to perform together. Courtney loved the idea of having both of them there on stage to back her up, but Riya's face went a sickly shade of yellow every time either of them brought it up. Her crippling stage fright, it seemed, had only gotten worse over the years.

"Oh, shoot," Riya said suddenly. "I have to call my parents and make sure they sent in my sports physical paperwork to my new coach at St. John's."

St. John's. The words echoed in her head. Courtney's blood turned to ice. Her steps faltered and she froze in place. Riya took two steps before she realized Courtney had stopped moving. She turned with a quizzical look on her face.

"Court, you look pale. You okay?"

Courtney took great pains to keep her voice calm and steady. "St. John's is the name of your new school?"

Riya nodded. "Yeah, they offered me a volleyball scholarship. It's a great school."

Courtney's stomach churned. "St. John's Academy in Charlotte?" Lots of schools were named St. John. Riya's school could be anywhere.

"Yes?" Riya said, making it sound like a question.

Courtney swore she felt capillaries in her brain explode.

"What's wrong, Courtney?"

Courtney's breath pulsed in and out of her lungs way too quickly. "Colt and I attend St. John's Academy in Charlotte."

St. John's only had high school students, so she hadn't attended there when she'd known Riya before. It was the best school in a hundred-mile radius, so Courtney and Colt drove thirty minutes into Charlotte every day to attend St. John's even though they lived just outside of Concord.

Next year, Riya and Courtney would be going to the same high school. They would be walking the same hallways and attending the same classes.

A smile inched across Riya's face. "We're going to be in high school together?"

Courtney watched the hope bloom across Riya's face and willed herself to feel the same way. She should feel the same way. Riya had made her happier in the past two weeks than she'd felt in a long time. Part of her wanted to continue that so desperately, she felt the desire like a magnetic pull. Instead, panic vanquished everything else.

Her summer fling, for better or for worse, was now so much more. Even with as much as she was coming to care for Riya, could she risk everything else to hold on to that? Her friends, her parents, her parents' friends—everyone could find out. But now that she'd rediscovered Riya, that she knew the heat of her skin and the buoyancy of her laugh, Courtney didn't want to give her up again.

Maybe they could continue on at St John's like they'd been at Pine Ridge. With both Colt's and Courtney's influence, they could integrate Riya into their group of friends so flawlessly no one would think twice about it. They'd have their stolen moments and after-school "study sessions" and maybe even sleepovers and it would be enough.

Until one of them slipped and someone found out.

They'd have to be so careful, meticulously discreet. But they could do it. They'd have to do it. Because, knowing what she knew now, Courtney didn't want to go back to denying herself the only kisses that'd ever meant anything.

Chapter Thirteen

At breakfast the morning after they'd realized they'd be attending the same school for senior year, Riya decided she wasn't imagining it: Courtney was freaked out. They'd told Dee the night before, but they'd also told Colt about St. John's. His joyful whoop contrasted sharply with Courtney's reaction. Last night, Courtney had crawled into Riya's bed as usual, but she'd just laid on Riya's shoulder, squeezing her tight until they both drifted off.

Courtney sat next to Riya and pushed her scrambled eggs around the plate with her fork, jumping every time Riya accidentally brushed her arm or leg. Halfway through the meal, she stood up without a word and walked away. She spent the rest of the time chatting with the young redheaded girl who'd taken a liking to her, Olivia.

Dee met Riya's eyes, concern swimming in the deep mahogany pools. When she'd told her, Dee was cautiously happy for Riya, glad for the relationship but worried about the secretiveness of it all. Dee was a pragmatist, which created a nice little spectrum in the most important people in Riya's camp life. Colt, the eternal optimist. Courtney, the pessimist and worrier. And Dee, right in the middle, telling it like it was.

After breakfast, Colt, Dee, Trey, Derek, and Riya continued their tradition of hiking while Bridget and Courtney cultivated their teenage boy fan club by lounging next to the pool, dipping in just long enough to cool off and to say they actually did some swimming. While hiking, their group had encountered a mama black bear with two cubs near a small river. They stood a respectful distance downstream, watching the creatures for a solid twenty minutes. The counselor leading the hike brought them far out of the way to circumvent the territorial bear, and they'd arrived a couple minutes after lunch was served. Talk of the bears dominated the table conversation, so Courtney's silence went unnoticed by everyone except Riya.

Finally, it was time for volleyball. Bridget, Courtney, and Elise lined up their towels next to one another and settled in to watch the games. Becky stood near the lake-side net pole, clipboard in hand and whistle at the ready. Bridget whispered something to Courtney, who laughed. Elise tried to join in, but she didn't know what they had been laughing about. Bridget frowned at her behind Courtney's back.

Riya threw herself into the sport. She focused on making the best of every single play, whether it was a perfect pass from Tiffany or a wild shank from Jenna, whose control had improved slightly since the first day. Saving wild balls was a part of the game, after all, just not usually as frequently as happened at Pine Ridge. Every time Riya started to get frustrated, she reminded herself it was good practice.

Four games in, Riya's breath pumped in and out of her chest and sand stuck to the sweat covering her entire body. Becky kept putting Jenna on Riya's team, to compensate. Riya was getting one heck of a workout.

The final game, the score was sixteen to seventeen and

Riya was serving. Derek saved one of David's slaps and lobbed the ball back over the net to Jenna. The ball bounced off of Jenna's knuckles and flew in Riya's direction, arcing to the outside. Riya dove for the ball, but she arrived a fraction of a second too late. The spinning ball glanced off the tip of her extended fist and zoomed parallel to the ground.

Riya watched the whole thing in slow motion. Courtney and Elise's mouths opened into perfect matching o-shapes as their eyes traced the ball's flight. Bridget was looking the other way, probably watching David on the other side of the court. The red and blue striped ball smacked against the left half of Bridget's forehead.

The girl screamed bloody murder. Riya looked up from her prone position on the sand. David rushed to Bridget's side. Riya resisted the urge to roll her eyes. She'd been smacked on the forehead dozens of times by balls hit much harder than that. It didn't even hurt that much, as long as it missed the nose and eyes.

"Are you okay, baby?" David said.

"No, I am not okay," Bridget shrieked, pointing a finger at Riya. "That dyke can't control herself."

The air on and around the court stilled. Elise gasped. Every pair of eyes bounced back and forth between Riya and Bridget. Riya stared straight at Courtney, waiting for her to say something. To stand up for her like she'd done so many times before. To tell Bridget she was out of line. Anything.

Courtney dropped Riya's gaze, then turned to examine the red mark on Bridget's forehead.

Riya's world imploded.

Her body went cold all over. Her heart stopped.

Dee, Stefanie, and Tiffany tensed, stepping forward. Colt strode in front of them, holding his hands out in supplication.

"Bridget," he said, admonishing. "That was rude and inappropriate."

"What?" Bridget said. "She hit me. She's a brute and a klutz."

Colt held up his hands in a frustrated gesture. "One, it was an accident and you know it. And two, it wouldn't have even happened if you got off your ass and actually played volleyball during, you know, volleyball."

Bridget's mouth dropped open.

"And three, that word is offensive."

Bridget shrugged. "It's true, though."

Elise scrambled to her feet, picking up her towel, and trotted over to join Stefanie. She distanced herself, physically, from Bridget.

Courtney did not.

Becky, who'd been watching with a horrified look on her face, finally regained her composure. She blew the whistle. "Okay, campers," she called, every ounce of her usual cheer absent. "It's time to head back and get ready for dinner."

Riya was the first to turn and walk away. Tiffany, Stefanie, Elise, and Dee caught up with her quickly. They ranted, calling Bridget terrible things, recounting past horribleness. Riya appreciated the solidarity, but tears sprang to her eyes as she replayed Courtney's actions—or lack thereof, more accurately.

Behind her, Riya heard Becky call, "Not you, Bridget. I need to talk to you."

Courtney did not show her face in the cabin as everyone readied for dinner. Riya's friends kept up a running commentary designed to cheer and distract her. Riya wanted to hug all of them.

In her mind, she kept hearing *that word* repeated over and over again. She kept seeing Courtney, turning away from her, refusing to defend her.

Courtney and Colt walked in to dinner late. Colt gave Riya a sad smile so full of sympathy and understanding it made her wish she'd fallen for the other Chastain sibling. It would've been so much easier.

Courtney's eyes were red and puffy. She hadn't even tried to cover the evidence with makeup. She sat at the end of the table, not looking at anything but the empty plate in front of her.

After dinner, everyone headed to the bonfire field for an evening of yard games like cornhole, ladder golf, and horseshoes. Riya let the tide of people sweep her up. People kept asking her to be their teammate for various games, and she complied every time. It gave her something to do, something else to think about besides Courtney, who hadn't made an appearance. Bridget and David stood separate from their usual group, a sour look on Bridget's face.

Bridget did not look apologetic in the least. Riya wondered if Courtney was sorry, if that was why she hadn't yet shown her face. And if it even mattered. How could there be any decent future for them when Riya couldn't count on Courtney to defend her from her own friends?

The alarmed look on Courtney's face when she realized they'd be going to the same school next year kept flashing through Riya's mind. Riya'd been thrilled at the news, hopeful. Courtney'd seemed shell-shocked. If Courtney meant all those thing she'd whispered in stolen moments over the past week, why didn't she share Riya's excitement?

"I'm going to head to bed," Riya whispered to Dee and Colt about thirty minutes before everyone else would turn in.

"I'll go with," Dee offered.

"No." Riya's voice was firm. She needed some time alone. "I'm exhausted. I'm just going to pass out."

Riya found Becky, telling her she didn't feel well and needed to go to bed.

"Is it because of what happened today?" Becky looked up at her with huge, sympathetic eyes.

Riya nodded. She *was* upset about something that had happened today, even if it wasn't exactly what Becky thought.

"I'm so sorry, Riya," Becky said. "I told Bridget how inappropriate it was."

Riya swallowed with difficulty. "Thanks. Is it all right if I go?"

Becky glanced at her watch, then looked over Riya's shoulder toward their cabin. Riya followed her gaze. From here, she could see about 90 percent of the path back to G7B.

"Yeah, go," Becky said in a breath. "We'll all be there in a little bit."

As Riya cleared the field, Colt jogged up next to her.

"Hey," he said.

"Hi," she said.

"Look, Riya. I'm sorry about today. Bridget's never been nice, but that was unacceptable."

Riya met his eyes, which glowed silver in the light from the full moon. Courtney's did the same. It seemed like everyone was apologizing to her except for the one person who really needed to. And she didn't mean Bridget.

"I don't care what Bridget said," Riya spat. And it was true. "I care that Courtney didn't defend me."

His head drooped, his chin falling toward his chest. "I know. And I know how hurt you are, but can I beg for leniency on her behalf?"

Riya raised an eyebrow. Her anger teetered on a knife's edge. If Colt hadn't been the one to defend her, she wouldn't have given him the benefit of the doubt.

"We had it out after volleyball," he said. "She feels terrible. She'll never admit it, but she's dealing with a lot of internalized self-loathing."

"You sound like a psychology textbook."

To her surprise, Colt grinned at that. "I took AP Psych last semester. Anyway, she's terrified. She's grown up in a culture that's brainwashed her into thinking every desire she's ever had is wrong. That she's broken. That she can fix herself if she tries hard enough."

"You grew up in that same culture, Colt."

He nodded. "Yeah, but they were never talking about me. It's much easier to separate yourself that way. Since they were talking about someone I loved, I could deny it."

"How long have you known?"

He shrugged. "Five, six years."

Riya's heart thumped in her chest. She stood still without saying anything.

"Yeah," Colt said, answering the question Riya hadn't asked. He knew because of Riya, because of the way Courtney acted around Riya.

Riya nodded. "Okay. I'll talk to her."

A warm smile spread slowly across his face. "Great, because she's waiting for you at the beach."

Riya's eyes widened. Colt shrugged.

Riya let out a single bark of a laugh. "Well, your parents can be happy they've got one shark in the family."

Colt held his hands over his heart. "You wound me."

Riya gave him a doubtful look before spinning on her heel.

Riya's speed fluctuated wildly as she walked. When she reached her cabin, she glanced back to see if anyone was watching her. Heart hammering in her chest, she passed it and kept walking. She alternated between hopeful and defeated, her steps accelerating and slowing with each mood swing. When she reached the beach, Courtney stood leaning against the lifeguard stand, staring out at the lake. Tears pricked at the corners of Riya's eyes. She blinked them back and swallowed the rising swell in her throat. Two years ago, Riya had sworn to herself that she'd no longer hide her true self, no matter how painful. Courtney had made her forget that promise. No more.

· · ·

Having given up on her hope that Riya would show, Courtney watched the tiny ripples in the lake's surface, trying to drown her thoughts in their miniscule crests. She'd have to head back in a couple minutes or Becky would notice her absence in the cabin. Courtney'd screwed up so badly that even Colt couldn't talk Riya into giving her a second chance.

Not that she deserved it.

Bridget'd called Riya that horrible word, and Courtney had literally turned her back on Riya. What the hell had she been thinking? Simple, she hadn't been thinking at all. Terror took control, shoving every decent thought into the backseat. Courtney was weak and she'd proven it today in front of everyone who mattered.

Courtney spun at the sound of a cough behind her. Riya stood next to a stack of canoes, her golden-brown skin glowing in the moonlight.

"You came." Courtney's voice lifted to an octave higher than usual.

"Yeah. Your brother is going to make a great lawyer one day," Riya explained.

Courtney stared at her hands. "My parents will be so proud."

Riya's feet shuffled forward, her movements unsure and hesitant. She used the momentum to walk past Courtney and sat on the sand, the toes of her flip-flops flirting with the waterline.

Courtney dropped down next to her. Words rushed out of her in a flood of regret. "I'm so sorry, Riya. I panicked. The very thing I'm afraid of was happening, and it was someone who was supposed to be my friend and I just froze."

Wordless, Riya continued staring at the rippling water. It reflected the full moon above like a distorted mirror.

"I'm sorry. What can I do?" Courtney slipped her hand into Riya's, punctuating her plea with squeezes. "Just tell me what to do and I'll do it."

Riya looked down at their clasped hands. "This," she said. "Hold my hand."

"Anyt—"

"At breakfast tomorrow. Walk in with me, holding hands."

Courtney felt all of the blood retreat from her face, leaving her cheeks cold and tingling. "I can't do that."

Courtney wanted to make Riya understand that today had been nothing, a lapse in judgment, a moment of overwhelming fear. But Riya didn't understand what she was asking Courtney to do.

Riya stood up. "Then I can't do this."

When Riya stood up, something inside Courtney snapped. She'd never been so scared on so many levels.

"I'm not ready, okay?" She stood. "Why can't you give me more time?"

Riya turned to face her. Tears streamed freely down her cheeks. They sparkled like diamonds in the moonlight. "I can't live a lie. I'm not like you."

The words hit Courtney like a boulder to her chest. "You think I'm a liar?"

"You lie to everyone around you. No one knows the real you, not even you. You can't really be honest with *yourself* unless you're drunk."

Courtney wanted to tell her that Riya knew the real her. That she'd shared things with Riya she'd never dreamed of telling anyone else. The moments they spent alone were the truest Courtney'd ever lived.

She reached out to grab Riya's wrist.

Riya yanked her hand away, raising it to tug on her ponytail, running her fingers through the thick strands all the way to the bottom.

Riya spoke. "I don't want to hide my feelings for you anymore, Courtney. I want to shout it from the rooftops. Don't you want that, too?"

The panic pumping through her blood intensified as she pictured it in her head. If it were just Pine Ridge, she might be able to deal with it. But now they were talking about St. John's, too. They were talking about her life. Her real life. Once the cat was let out of the bag, no one could put it back in again. If people knew... She couldn't.

After several seconds of Courtney not answering her question, Riya sobbed once.

"What is it?" Riya asked through angry tears. "Are you embarrassed of me? Am I not good enough to be with Courtney Chastain?"

Of course not. How could Riya think that? "You said you'd wait until I was ready to come out." She'd let Riya and Colt talk her into telling Dee, and Courtney'd been suffering minor panic attacks ever since, worrying Dee would say something to give her away.

"I'm done waiting," Riya said. "If you cared about me at all..."

Courtney's face flushed red and hot. Riya's words hit her like a punch to the stomach, and she took several steps back from her. For Riya to make Courtney's coming out about herself when she knew how much it might cost Courtney was more selfish than Courtney thought Riya capable of. "I just mean...we have something special, Courtney. Fate has gifted us the perfect chance." She motioned at the gorgeous moonlit lake like it was some sort of sign. "I'm going to your school next year. We could be great if you'd let us."

Absolutely not. It couldn't happen like that. Courtney had to stop this now. Riya would just keep pushing her to come out. Either way, it would have to end when they went home. She might as well end it tonight before either of them could get too attached. Before anyone could get too hurt.

"There is nothing special about *us*." The lie tasted bitter on her tongue.

Riya froze, her eyes growing so wide that they swallowed all the moonlight. "What are you saying?" Her voice cracked.

"Don't you get it?" Courtney spat.

She knew she sounded angry. Because she was. At her parents. At the world that was making her do this.

At herself.

"You're right," she continued. "I don't care about you. I'm experimenting. Rebelling before I have to go back home. You're willing. It's convenient." Courtney's stomach revolted against her words, threatening to toss up her dinner. She retreated until the lifeguard stand hit her back. She leaned against it, grateful for its support.

Maybe it was the way Riya's face crumpled in on itself, but Courtney swore she could literally hear Riya's heart breaking. As much as it ached, that's how Courtney knew she was doing the right thing. One more week of carrying on like they had been and Riya might shatter when it ended. Courtney might splinter into so many shards she'd never be able to put herself back together.

Riya's chest heaved. "Why are you doing this?"

She dug her nails into the wood at her back. One last lie and it would be over.

"Because you're more trouble than you're worth," Courtney said.

Riya's tears sparkled in the moonlight. Underneath them, her face went pale and creased with anger.

"You're a coward." There was a bitter bite to Riya's words. "Why don't you just run away, like you always do?"

Courtney pushed off the lifeguard tower and trudged through the sand, leaving Riya standing alone. For the third time.

For the last time.

Chapter Fourteen

Dee was livid. The twins and Elise were confused. Colt was unbearably sympathetic. Bridget was simply unbearable.

And Riya? Riya was… Well, it changed minute by minute. A day and a half after their fight at the beach, she still didn't know what to think or do most of the time.

When she woke up to find Courtney gone in the morning, she wondered how Courtney'd gotten permission to leave for practice without her. For Riya's part, she'd decided to skip morning practice from there on out. A couple of days' rest wasn't going to ruin her. And the extra hour of sleep did wonders for shrinking her puffy, red, cried-out eyes.

She told herself she'd put in a couple of extra hours once she got back home. Practicing with her parents returning the ball to her would be more productive than practicing alone anyway.

Not to mention, canceling the morning practices reduced her chances of running into Courtney alone to near zero. Worth it.

During the after-lunch rest period, Becky handed them

their mail. She had a small package from her parents with a couple pounds of her favorite candies—peanut butter cups and Almond Joys—and a long letter detailing all of their moving adventures. She smiled as she read it, realizing how much she'd missed them over the past several weeks. After tucking it away, she lay down and closed her eyes, trying to get a little rest. Getting to sleep at night, knowing Courtney lay only feet below her, had proven more than difficult.

Elise's laughter broke through the soft buzz of conversation. "He did not!" she said, then laughed again.

Someone else made a shushing sound.

Though the rest of them spoke quietly, Riya was now honed in on her friends' conversation at Dee's bunk. She didn't begrudge Dee her happiness with Colt, but she just couldn't handle that kind of talk right then. Quietly, Riya slid down the ladder to the floor and slipped her feet into flip-flops. As she walked out the door, she caught Dee looking at her. Her friend gave her a small nod and sympathetic smile.

She didn't really have an idea of where she was going, but she knew she couldn't stay in the cabin. Her next activity would be in the arts hut, so she headed in that direction, walking slowly and taking in the scenery. The majestic mountains, green forest, and sparkling lake were lovely, but part of Riya couldn't wait to get back to real civilization with internet and cell phone service and all of its virtual distractions.

When she approached the arts hut, she noticed movement inside the windows, and her steps stalled. Memories of her first day at Pine Ridge flashed through her brain, mixing with the image in front of her. Inside, Courtney twirled and leapt with singular grace, disappearing in the space between windows and bursting back into view.

Riya knew she should walk away. She wanted to. She just…couldn't. So she stood there under a cloudless mountain sky and watched Courtney dance.

"That's a little stalkery," Dee said from behind her.

Riya breathed a deep sigh as Dee stepped up to stand next to her.

"I'm going to have to get used to seeing her every day," Riya said. Thinking of walking down the same hallways as Courtney, maybe being in the same classes with her, was a knife twisting in her gut.

"You wanna talk about it?" Dee asked.

Riya hadn't yet told Dee everything, just that they'd fought and Courtney had broken up with her. She'd told herself the pain had been too new and raw to open up those wounds again, but part of her knew she didn't want to admit to Dee some of the things she'd said to Courtney.

Riya soaked up one last lingering glimpse and turned to stroll down the path past the boys' cabins. Dee followed.

"She doesn't care about me. She never did." Riya fought back the tears as she recounted Courtney's words. "I was her teenage experimentation."

"Did she actually say that?" Dee asked, her voice rising with disbelief.

Riya nodded. "She made it painfully unambiguous."

"Is that how she opened?" Dee asked. "Like, 'Hey, just kidding, I don't like you, I just wanted to try out some sweet, sweet lady kisses'?"

Riya's gaze dropped to her feet. "Not exactly." She gave Dee a full account of their fight. It was easy to remember, since she'd been replaying the words in her head every brutal moment. When she finished, Dee stayed quiet.

They passed another cabin and, still, Dee didn't comment.

"Okay, come on," Riya said. "What?"

"You want the truth?" Dee asked, raising an eyebrow at her while somehow squinting at the same time.

Riya's blood went cold. Dee regularly laid out painful truths without any warning, so if she thought Riya needed prior notification of this particular instance? Riya was not going to like it.

She took a deep breath, steeling herself. "Lay it on me."

"You might have pushed a little hard for her to come out," Dee said. "Her face went white as limestone when you told me. She's not ready. She wasn't ready."

"I don't want to force her to come out." Something squeezed tight in Riya's chest. "I don't."

"But you wanted her to publicly acknowledge you as her girlfriend?" Dee said.

Riya chewed on her bottom lip, not answering. That was what she had wanted, but Dee putting the two together made her realize what she'd been asking Courtney to do. Her stomach plummeted as a terrible sinking feeling crept across her torso.

"You do realize those two things cannot be mutually exclusive, right?" Dee said, her voice kind but firm. "If she holds your hand, if she kisses you, she's out. I mean, you're not an idiot, so I know you understand that on some level, at least."

Riya blew out a breath and buried her face in her hands.

"You have a great support system and had a relatively easy coming out, and that's super awesome," Dee said, placing a hand on her back. "But Courtney's will not be so easy. She's terrified, and she has every right to be. You basically told her your feelings were more important than hers."

Tears welled in Riya's eyes. "Okay, okay, I get it." She held up a hand. "I'm the worst." Her heart wrenched when she thought about how Courtney must have felt—like Riya's desire to be acknowledged was more important than Courtney's need to feel safe.

Dee bumped Riya with her shoulder. "So do you think that she meant it? That she didn't care about you? Or do you think she felt trapped?"

Riya hadn't even considered that Courtney hadn't been telling the truth about her feelings that night or since. She looked over her shoulder, but sun glinted off the arts hut windows and she couldn't see anything from that distance. It didn't matter. Courtney had made one thing perfectly clear in the last thirty-six hours: she did not want to talk to Riya ever again.

· · ·

Courtney spent every free second working on her dance. It was the only reason she hadn't called her parents to come get her the night she left Riya alone on the beach. She just had to perform flawlessly in front of David's dad and hope he saw something special in her.

She avoided Riya, changing her schedule to activities she knew Riya hated. Any time they were forced to be in the same room, Courtney ignored Riya like her life depended on it. So far, so good. Mostly.

Courtney barely slept. She tossed and turned all night until her alarm went off. She missed those stolen hours with Riya, and she missed the friendships she'd made with Stefanie, Elise, and Dee, who wouldn't speak to her. And after she'd told Bridget off for being so mean to her *friend* Riya, Courtney had no one else. She'd started at the top of the social food chain and now she was nothing.

And she didn't care.

It was liberating. She didn't do her makeup if she didn't feel like it. She didn't strategically time her entrances or her outfits for maximum effect. She went through her days without wondering what anyone else thought of this action or that statement.

Colt regularly stopped in to check on the dance's progress. He tried to talk to her about Riya, but she flat-out refused every time. If she didn't talk about or look at Riya, then Riya didn't exist. Then Courtney's feelings for her didn't exist.

The day before the talent show—the day before they would go home—Courtney and Colt conducted a dress rehearsal before breakfast. Colt played the piano while Courtney adjusted her dance to the confines of the cafeteria "stage." She'd practiced so much over the last couple of weeks that she no longer had to think about what came next. The dance flowed effortlessly and she loved how the live piano instilled elegance and panache.

The last echoes of the music dissipated.

"It's incredible," Colt said, awed.

"Really?" Courtney asked. "You don't think it's too… maudlin?"

Colt laughed. "Only you would think a ballet set to Adele could possibly be too emotional. It's perfect."

She sat on a bench to untie the laces of her ballet shoes. "It has to be," she murmured. Imminent dread had crept up on her over the past week. Though she knew she had so much ahead of her, she couldn't help feeling like tomorrow would be her last chance.

Colt dallied on the piano, slipping seamlessly from song to song, crafting an accidental melody.

She pulled a pair of flip-flops and a sweater from her tote and slipped them on, tucking the ballet shoes in the bag. Courtney tossed the bag under her seat at the end of her cabin's table.

The notes slowed and then stopped. Colt's fingers rested lightly over the keys. He watched her closely in that way that promised trouble.

"You're not going to take your stuff back to your cabin?" Colt asked.

Courtney blinked, then glared at him. He knew better. Courtney'd been doing an excellent job of avoiding Riya, leaving in the morning before she woke and returning at the last possible second every night.

He sighed and stood. "What are you going to do when we go back to school?" he said. "She'll be there."

Courtney's heart erupted into a salsa beat, but she kept her face stoic. "It's not like we're going to run in the same circles. She's a jock *and* a scholarship kid."

"She's my friend, too, you know," Colt reminded her, as if she'd been able to forget with her, him, and Dee spending every waking second together. "You can't keep me from hanging out with her."

"Traitor."

Colt looked at the ceiling and blew air out in a noisy raspberry. He was annoyed with her.

"What do you expect me to do, Colt? The daughter of Chastain and Chastain cannot parade around St. John's Academy with a girlfriend on her arm."

Colt's eyes turned sad. "That's the problem. You are not the daughter of Chastain and Chastain. You're something better. You are *Courtney Chastain*. You can be whoever you want to be. You can do whatever you want."

It wasn't so simple. It could never be that simple. Why was she the only one who saw that? "You're naive."

He studied her for several seconds. "Maybe, but you're a cynic. And it's going to cost you the only other person in the world who truly knows you and loves you anyway."

Loves you. The words scored themselves across her skin. Because in the days before their fight, Courtney had been so close to saying those words a hundred times.

Heat flared across Courtney's face and in her chest. "I'm a realist. It's not my fault I actually see things for how they are."

Colt tucked in the piano bench, then strolled over to kneel in front of her. "Courtney, I love you. All I've ever wanted for you is happiness. And for two weeks, for the first time in a long while, you had it. I saw it. Don't be mad at me for wanting to see that again."

The silence stood between them as Courtney searched for something to say to make him understand.

Colt intruded on her thoughts. "Don't *you* want that again?"

Courtney forced a breath through pursed lips. "Colt. I just…can't. Our parents—"

"Have nothing to do with this," Colt interrupted.

He was starting to get angry. He wasn't the one who should be angry. Courtney was the one getting grilled and accused.

She turned to pick up her bag, but Colt placed his hands on her shoulders, bringing her attention back to him. "You know I'm going to support you no matter what you do. I will never tell you how to live your life. Just…don't let anyone else. Especially Mother and Father."

"Mom threatened to cut me off if I went to Juilliard. What do you think they'd do if I brought home a girlfriend?"

It was so easy to talk with Colt about things that made her feel like the sky might fall down around her when she pondered them alone. He was that way with everyone; it was his gift. It seemed like all Courtney could do was make other people feel worse about their insecurities. She hoped that wasn't her gift.

Colt waved his hands. "Forget everything outside of you. Does your heart speed up when she looks at you?"

Courtney bit her lip, refusing to even consider the question. "That's not…" She trailed off weakly.

He nodded once. "Does your skin tingle long after she's touched you?"

Courtney felt the ghost of hundreds of shivers on her skin. She clutched her arms around her waist, suppressing them.

"Court," he pleaded with her. "Do you love her?"

Courtney swallowed. She did not answer. She did not even acknowledge the answer to herself.

Either her lack of denial spoke volumes or Colt saw something in her face, because he raised his palms up in an agitated gesture. "That's it, that's all you need. Jesus, that is *it*. If you have that, everything is possible."

She shook her head. "It's impossible."

"No." He stood up. "It's hard."

"Exactly!" She gestured back at him.

"But let me tell you the secret: all relationships are hard. They all come with their unique challenges. And most of them aren't even worth it. But someone like Riya doesn't come along every day. The universe handed you a second chance on a silver platter. Don't waste it."

Courtney had never been a big believer in fate—"meant to be" was such a cliché—but neither did she put much stock in coincidences. Riya was here, in the summer camp Courtney had been attending since she was a child. And starting in August, Riya and Courtney would be in the same building every weekday for nine months. Courtney had to wonder if that meant something, if it was a sign.

Or maybe it was one big cosmic joke.

Chapter Fifteen

The last few days at camp, Riya had finally gotten back into the swing of things. Every time she saw Courtney, her heart squeezed painfully, but she focused on making the most of the last few days in a beautiful place with some of the best friends she'd ever had. At lunch the second to last day, they ate pizza and took hundreds of selfies with each other.

Courtney sat on the other end of the table with Jenna and Kanda, and Riya was doing an excellent job of pretending she didn't exist.

The small redhead, Olivia, marched up to Courtney, arms crossed.

"Who hurt you?" Olivia demanded. She looked ready to brawl on Courtney's behalf.

Courtney shook her head. "No one. I hurt someone else," Courtney said, her voice thick and scratchy.

The girl's tiny features twisted in confusion. "Why are you so sad, then?"

"Because I wish I hadn't."

Riya's heart did somersaults in her chest. She raised her

head to openly watch the interaction, but Courtney didn't notice.

Olivia considered that for a couple seconds, face scrunched up in confusion. "So apologize." She said it, just like that. As if it were so simple. As if a couple words could make up for the betrayal Courtney'd perpetrated.

Courtney gave her a small smile. "I think it's too late."

"My grandma told me it's never too late to apologize," Olivia said.

"Your grandma might be right. Thanks, Liv."

The girl nodded and trotted back to her table, confident in her simplistic worldview. Riya envied her. Courtney went back to ignoring Riya, and Riya went back to pretending like it didn't hurt.

Later that afternoon, Riya and her friends gamboled from the art hut to the courts for the last day of volleyball at Pine Ridge. How fitting that their last artsy session had included weaving embroidery thread together to create friendship bracelets. Each girl's wrist sported a five-strand braid of red, blue, purple, white, and pink. One color to represent each of them.

Their laughter echoed across the lake, loud and boisterous, chasing away any sorrow about their impending separation.

Dee's face blazed with happiness the second she spotted Colt warming up with some of the other players. She ran up to him, throwing her arms around his waist. He wrapped her in a bear hug. Dee's feet lifted several inches off the sand, and she squealed with delight. Colt planted a noisy, showy kiss square on Dee's mouth.

Riya scanned the area, telling herself she wasn't searching for Courtney. She was making sure Courtney wasn't there. Totally different.

Riya'd only seen Courtney at mealtimes, but at night, Riya laid awake until she heard Courtney settle in below her.

Every night, she fantasized about feeling that shifting weight on her mattress, but it never came.

Riya knew Dee was right. Her expectations had been unreasonable for someone so scared of her truth being exposed to the world. But on the other hand, wasn't it unfair of Courtney to expect Riya to keep hiding, pretending, and lying to her friends? Riya couldn't decide who was to blame for their collapse. Maybe it was both their faults. Maybe it was neither.

Either way, she tried to focus on what she did have. Beautiful Blue Ridge Mountain weather, awesome friends, and volleyball every other day.

To Riya's surprise, Elise joined the bump circle instead of going directly to her usual spot. Stefanie stared at her, open-mouthed.

Elise shrugged. "Last chance, right?"

As people arrived, the teams formed naturally with a little guidance from Tiffany, who made sure talent was evenly distributed. She instructed Stefanie and Riya to stay with Elise, placing David and Jenna on her own team. That was not a good sign for Elise's gameplay.

Becky whimpered before blowing the whistle to start the game. "I'm going to miss you guys so much."

Some days their games were competitive and some days they were less so. Today, the atmosphere was downright silly. Elise's volleyball skills were, as advertised, quite terrible, but she tried. People tackled each other in the sand for missing easy balls. Even the twins relaxed, sending perfect sets over with lazy slaps instead of hard-driven spikes.

It was fun.

Until the last five minutes.

Halfway through the final game of the summer, Jenna hit the ball and, predictably, it went wide. Derek and Colt dove at the same time, hands outstretched. With their torsos and flailing limbs between the ball and her, Riya couldn't see the impact. But she heard the unmistakable thud of fingers hitting the ball at a totally wrong angle.

Colt cried out in pain. He rolled over onto his back, his left hand clutching his right.

Riya dashed to his side, placing a comforting palm on his shoulder.

"Dude, are you okay?" Derek rubbed a hand across his jaw. "I'm so sorry."

Riya looked up at him. "What happened?"

"I hit the ball a nanosecond before he did. I think it jammed his fingers."

"Go get some ice in a bag," she said. "And a towel. Run."

Derek nodded and sprinted toward the cafeteria.

Riya turned her attention back to Colt. Becky joined her on Colt's other side, fumbling with a first-aid kit.

"Let me see." Riya tugged his left wrist until he released his injured hand.

Dee knelt next to Riya on the sand, running soothing fingers up and down his left forearm and biceps.

"Which finger is it?" Riya asked. She'd jammed plenty of fingers going after the same ball as someone else over the years. It hurt like hell but usually healed in a couple of days.

Colt pointed at the base of both the middle and ring fingers on his right hand.

Riya examined them. They stretched out long and straight with no odd bends or kinks. That was good, at least. But Colt's face crumpled with pain when she prodded with a gentle finger.

She reached across Colt to riffle through the first-aid kit. She pulled out a roll of one-inch-wide medical tape. With Becky's cautious help, Riya taped his middle finger to his index and his ring finger to his pinkie.

"Don't move them more than you absolutely have to.

This is called buddy taping. It helps to keep the injured fingers immobile."

Colt's eyes went wide. "Can I play piano?"

Riya shook her head. "Probably not. If they swell and turn red in the next couple of minutes, they might be broken."

Breathing rapidly, Derek returned with a quart-size Ziploc bag filled with ice and a small white towel.

Riya wrapped the towel around the bag of ice and pressed it against the back of Colt's hand. "Fifteen minutes of ice every hour for two days. If it starts hurting a lot, try raising it above your heart. The tape is structural, so replace it whenever it becomes…not."

Behind her, Elise said, "Look at Riya! She's like a doctor or something."

Riya shook her head, laughing. "When you're a klutz who plays a sport, you learn first aid pretty quickly."

"Does he need a real doctor?" Dee asked.

Riya met Colt's panicked eyes before answering. "Maybe."

Becky offered a hand down to his uninjured hand. Colt stared at it. Derek slipped his hands under Colt's underarms and pulled him to a standing position.

"Let's go see the nurse," Becky told him. "She'll decide whether you need to go into town or not."

Derek grabbed Colt's water bottle from the sidelines. "I'll go with you."

Colt spun back toward Riya, gesturing with a jerk of his head for Dee to come closer.

"Do not tell Courtney," he ordered.

"Why?" Riya asked. She deserved to know that her brother was hurt.

"She'll get so mad at us," Dee added.

"It doesn't matter." Colt's voice was scared, but not for himself. He was scared for his sister. "If I'm not back by dinner, make something up. Tell her Derek got hurt and I'm going with him to the doctor."

"Colt—" Riya began.

His eyes pierced hers in an uncomfortably familiar way. He was trying to convey something without words. "She cannot know, not tonight. She needs to sleep tonight thinking everything's okay."

The talent show. The scholarship. Colt was supposed to play piano while Courtney danced tomorrow morning.

"It may be nothing," Colt said. "A shot or something and I might be able to play. Until we know otherwise, nobody says a word to Courtney."

"Let's go," Becky said. Her big eyes stared at Colt's hand, which swelled more and more by the second. The skin between the strips of tape turned a bright shade of red.

"I don't understand," Riya said. "Can't she just dance to the recording? That's how she practiced."

Colt shook his head. "She'll freak. She thinks she's cursed or something. Just don't let her know. I'll take care of it."

Becky tugged on his good arm, and he relented. Derek followed closely behind them, repeatedly apologizing and offering his help.

The rest of the volleyball players strolled in silence to their cabins to prepare for the final night's celebrations.

At dinner, Courtney kept scanning the room, her brow wrinkled. She stared at Dee, trying to catch her attention, but Dee studiously ignored her.

Riya took pity on her. She slid down the bench until she sat across from Courtney.

Courtney tried to look anywhere except at Riya but surrendered after a couple of awkward seconds.

"Do you know where he is?" Courtney asked.

Riya remembered Colt's insistence that his sister not know about his injury. But she had to tell Courtney something, so she borrowed his suggested lie. "He had to go to the hospital."

Courtney's skin turned a pallid shade of white, the same color as hospital walls. "Wha—what?" Her jaw clenched and unclenched.

Colt had been right. Finding out her brother had been injured would unhinge her after all the pressure she'd put herself under.

Riya exhaled. "He's okay," she lied. "He went to help Derek."

Courtney's shoulders relaxed, but she still refused to meet Riya's gaze.

Riya felt like a fraud. She took advantage of Courtney's lack of eye contact and stared at the table as she spoke. "He may not be home until late. He said to tell you not to worry."

"Should I go, too?" Courtney fidgeted in her seat. "I should go, right?"

"No!" Riya nearly screeched the word. She gripped the bench beneath her legs and tried again. "No. I…uh. I don't think Derek would want you there."

Courtney pressed her lips together and nodded, dropping her gaze to her plate. "Oh. Yeah. Probably not."

Guilt stabbed Riya's gut. She hadn't meant to reopen old wounds. "No, it's not that," she said. "It's just that the injury is in a, you know, sensitive area."

Courtney's pale skin blushed a stunning shade of pink.

Riya wanted to kick herself. That night on the lake, she'd told Courtney she wasn't a liar. *Now look at me.*

Courtney continued to stare at her plate. Riya wanted to say something. She kept coming up with things in her head to say, then rejecting them. *I'm looking forward to seeing you dance*, only reminded her of the hours they'd spent alone while Courtney practiced. *So what classes are you taking next semester?* would only freak Courtney out more. *I hope we can be friends next year.* Did that sound too desperate?

Riya settled on, "Good luck tomorrow."

Courtney raised her head and held Riya's gaze for two eternal seconds. Something flashed deep within their aquamarine depths. Something Riya couldn't identify.

"Thanks," Courtney said.

Riya slid back across the wooden bench to rejoin her friends, feeling the resuming distance between them more acutely than she had since their fight.

. . .

Courtney opted to skip out on the last-night festivities in order to run through her dance a couple more times. Colt had said it was perfect, but Courtney knew there wasn't such a thing as too much practice. If she practiced enough, the movements became second nature, and then her conscious mind could focus on infusing the dance with true passion.

She spun and leapt across the wooden floor of the arts hut, wishing Colt were there to practice with her. She'd listened to the song so many times that she heard it in her sleep, as soon as she woke up, and every night as she drifted off. The minor key, the soulful vocals, and the words so full of regret and longing had formed the background of her life for the last week.

But hearing the instrumental version on the piano that morning as she danced had transformed her performance, and it no longer felt complete without the live music.

Dancing without the lyrics would be a relief. Every time she heard the line *It's me*, she had to wipe away the image of Riya listening on a phone in a couple of years, refusing to respond to any of Courtney's pleas. She'd always wondered why the singer felt they were both running out of time, but now it made sense. Because every day neither of them made a move back to each other, it became that much harder to even imagine that they could.

Courtney slipped off her ballet shoes and slipped on some flip-flops. Her toes were bruised and beaten. After tomorrow's performance, she promised her aching feet she'd take a short break to let some of the blisters heal.

She walked back to the cabin in blissful silence. Above her, the sky was still a dark orange from the setting sun and some of the brightest stars were already starting to make their nightly debut. When she entered the cabin, it was empty. Everyone must've still been at the last-night-at-camp party.

She decided to get a head start on tomorrow's packing. She very studiously ignored Riya's crumpled bed, small pieces of fabric sticking out of Riya's drawers, her smell all around their bunk. Riya was everywhere.

She found herself staring at a pair of Riya's volleyball shorts draped over the top rail of Riya's bed. When her stomach lurched, Courtney told herself she was only nervous about tomorrow.

Girls started filtering back in before they were both ready for bed. Riya and her friends came stumbling in, drunk on laughter.

Dee leaned in and whispered something to Riya, who nodded in response.

"I'm okay," she said.

Well, that made one of them.

She lost herself in all her cabin mates' excited chatter as everyone prepared for bed. Courtney crawled into bed and listened to Tiffany, Dee, and Riya make plans to visit each other before school started. In the far corner, Elise and Stefanie sat cross-legged across from each other on Elise's bed. Murmurs from their conversation clanged like soft bells during quiet lulls. Courtney thought it was the quietest she'd ever heard Elise's voice.

Girls climbed into their beds one by one and conversation settled down to soft whispers. Courtney closed her eyes and took deep breaths, attempting to calm her racing heart enough to sleep.

A knock sounded on the door. Courtney's eyes popped open. Tiffany's bed was closest, so she hopped up and crossed the room in a couple long strides, flinging the door open.

"Dee," she called.

Dee slipped down from her bed above Elise's and bounded to the door.

"Hey," she said. "How are you?" It wasn't a casual question. Courtney could tell there was meaning behind it.

"Hey, I'm okay. It's good to see you," Colt said. Courtney heard the smack of a quick kiss. "But I'm actually here to see my sister."

Riya slid down the ladder before Courtney climbed out from underneath her covers. Riya beat her to the door.

"How are you?" she said, breathless with worry.

Colt caught sight of Courtney over Riya's head. "I'm fine," he said. "I also need to talk to you after I talk to my sister, so wait up, okay?"

Colt jerked his head toward outside so Courtney would follow him.

"I have good news and bad news," Colt said.

They strolled toward the lake.

Courtney raised her head to stare at the sky. Those stars she'd glimpsed earlier had been joined by hundreds of their friends. "What's the good news?"

"Mom and Dad are coming tomorrow for the talent show."

Courtney's muscles tensed. "And what's the good news?"

Colt let out a small laugh.

"Why would they be coming?" They'd never come before. Her heart hammered painfully against her ribs. Maybe they knew about the scholarship and were coming to stop her from dancing.

"Because of the bad news." Colt stopped and turned to face her, running his left hand through his hair.

That's when she noticed the splints—plural—on his right hand.

"Colt!" Courtney grabbed his wrist and stared at the contraptions. "What happened?"

"I got hurt during volleyball."

Courtney threw her hands up in the air. "Who knew volleyball was such a dangerous sport?"

"I had to go to urgent care, so Fozzie Bear called our parents."

"How bad is it?" She peered at his hand but couldn't see much beyond the contraptions and tape.

"Each finger has a small stress fracture. They'll heal fine as long as I keep them immobile for about a month."

"Ouch," she said.

Immobile. The word pecked at her brain.

Courtney's breath came fast until she felt on the verge of hyperventilating. "You can't play the song tomorrow, can you?"

"Not exactly. But don't worry, okay? I have it covered. It's going to be even better."

"What do you mean 'don't worry'?" Something roared in Courtney's ears. "This is one of the most important performances of my entire life. I can't do it to an mp3 on a freaking staticky boom box."

"You won't have to, I promise." Colt's words spilled out in a rush. "Just trust me. This once. Let me handle it."

"Colt. I—"

"Don't you trust me?"

He had her there. If she argued, it meant she didn't trust him. But the fact that he wouldn't tell her his plan made her stomach twist into painful knots.

"I've got it under control," he said. "It's going to be great,

I promise. Just try to get some sleep so you're not all black-eyed tomorrow."

He walked her back to the cabin. Two hours later, she finally fell into a fitful sleep.

Chapter Sixteen

Riya twisted the fingers of both hands together until it hurt. She sat in the cafeteria at their usual table with Dee on one side and Tiffany on the other. How in the world had Colt talked her into this? Of course, it hadn't really been that hard. "Courtney needs you," he'd said. She would've said yes to anything that followed that statement and Colt knew it.

Jerk.

They'd cleared the area where they usually picked up food to create a makeshift stage. All the campers sat at their usual tables while chairs littered any open space for the parents who'd come early to watch. Somewhere among the crowd sat David's dad, the reason for this whole mess. He better be worth it.

Courtney's parents had arrived after the talent show began, so they stood in the back. Every time Riya glanced back at them, Mrs. Chastain typed on her phone.

Riya's parents were scheduled to arrive around lunch time, since Riya hadn't planned on participating in the talent show. She'd seen no reason to call them and make them change their plans.

On the stage, a very young-looking girl played the violin. Riya was pretty sure it wasn't supposed to screech like that every other note, but she had the basic melody down so that was something.

Courtney would be the final competitor. After her past dominance, Riya guessed no one wanted to perform after her.

Riya twisted in her seat through a juggler who was fantastic, a singer who was decent, and a comedian who was neither.

Becky appeared on the stage. "And now, we have the final Camp Pine Ridge performance of a long-time favorite, Courtney Chastain."

Most people applauded politely. Trey and David whooped. The little girl Olivia screamed like Becky'd announced her favorite pop star would be performing.

Colt walked over to the piano. It had been placed in the back corner of the stage area. He pushed up the hinged wooden piece that covered the keys with his left hand and sat, nodding to Riya.

Riya stood. Good, her knees didn't give out from the shaking.

"What are you doing?" Dee hissed, but Riya kept walking.

She focused only on Colt, with his encouraging smile, sure she'd puke if she looked at anything else that made her think about what she was walking up to do.

But as she made her way, a flash of blond on the side of the stage caught her attention, and she veered toward Courtney. Courtney stared at her, open-mouthed.

"I just want to say," Riya whispered, glancing over her shoulder at the curious crowd. "I'm so sorry. I pushed you and I shouldn't have. Please accept this as my apology." She spun away and resumed her path to Colt.

"What?" Courtney said from behind her, but Riya didn't

turn around again.

She reached the piano and pressed her hips into the gentle curve between the wider and narrower portions, as if she might disappear into it.

After a couple seconds of hesitation and confusion, Courtney floated onto the stage area in nude tights and a lavender leotard with a small matching skirt tied at the hip. There were no spotlights in the cafeteria, but Riya could've sworn a glowing light followed Courtney across the floor.

When Courtney turned to look at Colt, her gaze landed on Riya. She flinched. Her blue eyes flashed anger at Colt. She was upset he hadn't told her the plan, but he shrugged. They all knew Courtney would've rejected his idea even though it was, by far, Courtney's best shot.

"Ready?" Colt said to Riya.

"As I'll ever be."

They'd practiced a few times early that morning before breakfast. Colt had modified the piano part so he could play with his left hand and one finger of his right hand, but he couldn't play the full song with the melody representing the vocals like that. And Riya had heard the song so many times during Courtney's practices that she barely needed any preparation at all.

"It only makes sense," Colt had said last night.

Right.

Courtney shook her head and got into her starting position. Riya could see the exact second her mind switched to performance mode. Her legs were crossed, her head bowed. Her arms were wrapped tightly around her chest, her fingers pressing into her back.

Riya clutched her hands together in front of her.

"Six. Seven. Eight," Colt said under his breath.

The precise moment he played the first note, Courtney's head rose. Her arms stretched out, forming an elegant, straight line at an angle to the ground.

Four notes in, Riya took a breath. *Do not look at the crowd, do not look at anyone,* she told herself. With hundreds of eyes on her, pretending they didn't exist was the only way she was going to get through the song. The fingernails of her right hand cut into the palm of her left.

"Hello," she sang. It came out tight and slightly sharp. She looked at Courtney to see if she'd noticed. If she messed Courtney up, with so much on the line, Riya would die right there on that stage in front of everyone.

But Courtney moved flawlessly.

New plan: Watch Courtney. She was the reason Riya was doing this, the only reason Riya could do this.

"It's me," Riya sang. When she watched Courtney, everything else faded away. The stage fright dissipated. She could pretend they were in the art hut, Riya singing along with the tinny sound coming from Courtney's little speaker.

As she continued to sing the penitent words, Riya didn't take her eyes off of the fluid, willowy girl who moved across the floor as though it were the Lincoln Center in New York.

When Riya belted out the chorus, murmurs drifted up to her from her own table, but she still didn't look away. Courtney leapt so high, Riya worried her outstretched arm might smack against the ceiling. Her feet landed on the tile floor as soft as a feather.

Riya had seen this dance a hundred times, but this was different. This was art in motion. A hush fell over the crowd. They knew they sat in the presence of greatness.

The concluding piano notes faded. Courtney held her final pose.

The audience erupted. Kids and adults shouted, but Olivia was still the loudest—louder even, if it were possible, than Elise.

Riya tore her gaze away from Courtney and found her

parents leaning against the back wall. Mr. and Mrs. Chastain stared open-mouthed at Courtney. Riya wondered how long it had been since either of them attended one of her performances. Mrs. Chastain dabbed at her eyes with a tissue.

Courtney took her bows with all the grace she'd exhibited during the dance. Colt came up next to Riya, taking her hand and leading her to the center of the stage. He kept his grip firm when she tried to pull away. Colt bowed, then raised his injured hand to indicate Riya.

The crowd exploded once more. Riya stared awestruck at the reaction. Then, all of a sudden, slender arms wrapped around her shoulders from behind.

She turned and raised her head to find Courtney there, grinning and squeezing her. "Thank you."

Riya grinned back.

Courtney punched her brother playfully on the shoulder. "You sly bastard."

He rubbed his arm, wincing then laughing. "It's not nice to beat up on injured people."

Courtney punched him again.

The applause died down and had almost stopped when Courtney grabbed Riya's hand and raised it high in the air. She bowed low and framed Riya with a graceful gesture. The applause revived and Courtney's grin stretched as wide as Riya'd ever seen it.

Courtney spun in front of Riya, slipping her free hand behind her waist and pulling her. Her momentum turned Riya ninety degrees until they stood face-to-face, their sides to the crowd in a couple-dancing position.

"Riya, do you still like me?" Courtney whispered, her face suddenly serious. "In that way?"

Riya creased her brow. "Yes," she answered automatically before remembering she wasn't supposed to admit that.

The corners of Courtney's mouth twitched. She stood

frozen for a moment.

"Courtney?"

"Do you think you might love me? Or could, one day?"

Riya felt a lump the size of a golf ball in her throat. Her limbs went numb as she realized it was finally time for the truth. "I know I do. Now."

"And if I love you, if I want to try again, would you wait for me to be ready?"

Riya felt the sting of tears in the corners of her eyes. "As long as you need me to."

In a smooth movement, Courtney released Riya's waist to cup her face in her clammy hand. She leaned forward, pulling Riya toward her. A gasp sounded in the crowd.

"I'm ready."

Then, Courtney planted a kiss on Riya's lips that left no room for interpretation. Riya's eyes fluttered closed and she melted into Courtney's embrace. The audience faded into nothingness. Nothing else in the world existed except for Courtney, Riya, and the tiny pockets of space between their bodies. The kiss felt like a promise, like an oath offered right there in front of everyone.

In front of Courtney's parents. Riya's eyes burst open at the thought. Courtney ended the kiss and offered Riya a shaky smile.

"Courtney?" Riya said again. Was this actually happening? Riya pulled in several deep breaths. She couldn't get enough oxygen, no matter how hard she tried.

"I don't want to lie anymore," she said. "About anything. Not to you. Especially not to myself."

Riya smiled. An electric thrill shot through her body.

Courtney slid her arm into Riya's and hooked her brother's elbow on the other side before walking them off the stage.

. . .

By the time Becky announced the winner of the talent show, Courtney shook so badly she couldn't walk up to collect her trophy without Colt's help. What had she done? It had felt so incredibly right in the moment, in the afterglow of the applause and the high of a perfect performance. Riya's bravery was contagious. She'd overpowered crippling stage fright to help Courtney dance the best performance of her life. Riya's fearlessness had inspired her, infected her. Riya had done the thing that scared her more than anything else. For her. Courtney wanted to do the same.

But then she'd stepped into the audience, dozens of shocked gazes watching her, and panic set in. The attention struck her like a steady stream of cannonballs lobbed from a hundred tiny ships.

She couldn't even look at her parents yet. At least they hadn't marched down to where Riya, Colt, and Courtney sat on the floor together and snatched her away. She chose to take it as a good sign.

Courtney leaned against Colt, clutching his good hand as she accepted the trophy and offered the crowd one last shaky bow. She kept her eyes on Riya, refusing to look anywhere else.

Each counselor took a minute or two to say good-bye to the room before everyone was released. When the collective sound of people rising from their chairs rose, Courtney squeezed Colt and Riya's hands to keep herself from sprinting away.

"I already have one broken hand," Colt said. "You want to complete the set?"

Riya stood, pulling Courtney to her feet.

"You okay?' she whispered. Her big brown eyes swam with concern, but without a trace of fear. If only Courtney could borrow some of Riya's courage for today.

People began to move and Courtney braced for it, her entire body going so tense she thought her muscles might snap like rubber bands. A couple parents of younger children rushed over and guided their kids quickly out the door, frowning back at her. Riya tugged on Courtney's arm, bringing her attention to Trey, who stood in front of them.

"Awesome dance, Court," Trey said, patting her on the back. He turned to Riya. "And you were incredible."

Riya's eyes drifted down to his shoulder. "Thanks."

More campers came up to them. Every time, she readied herself for some terrible comment about the kiss. Every time, they congratulated her on her performance. A tall, wide-shouldered man who rocked gray hair and a suit like George Clooney approached her.

"Nathan Burns." He stuck out his hand for Courtney to shake.

She obliged. "Nice to meet you," she said politely, not sure why this man was introducing himself.

To his left and halfway across the room, a familiar face caught her attention. Bridget's scowl stared back at her. Courtney couldn't bring herself to care at the meaning behind it, and she refocused on the man in front of her.

He flashed a quick smile. "I'm David's father. You know David, right?"

Breath rushed from Courtney's lungs. "Yes, of course."

"Your brother told me you're applying to Juilliard," he said, nodding at Colt.

Colt had been busy, it seemed.

"I don't know if you know about the Riverdrake scholarship? I'm president of the Board of Directors there."

Courtney shook her head, then nodded, then shook her head again. "No. Yes. I mean, of course I know about it."

He smiled, perfect white teeth flashing. "Good. I'll keep

an eye out for your application then?" It was a question, but the kind of question powerful people asked knowing the only possible answer was yes.

Courtney nodded, her head bobbing up and down uncontrollably. "Definitely. Thank you." Words failing her, she resisted the urge to say "thank you" over and over again.

Then, Nathan Burns turned to Riya. Courtney's heart leapt into her throat.

"And what about you?" he asked her. "You'll be studying Vocal Performance, I'm assuming?"

Within a second, Riya's face turned bright red. "No. Oh, no. I'll be doing pre-med. Thank you, though."

He shrugged, a casually elegant gesture. "Shame." He flashed another quick smile. "It was lovely meeting you two ladies. Best of luck."

Then he was gone.

"Ohmigod," Courtney squealed.

Riya hugged her. She wasn't the type to squeal with Courtney, but she rocked back and forth with her.

Riya's friends filled the hole left by Mr. Burns. Stefanie cleared her throat and Riya released her.

Courtney chewed her lip as the silence stretched on.

"It's about freaking time," Dee said, backhanding Courtney's biceps.

Tiffany, Stefanie, and Elise nodded in agreement.

"Seriously," Stefanie said.

Courtney's chest filled with gratitude. She wanted to yank them all into a huge group hug, but Colt elbowed her.

She looked up to find him staring over Tiffany's shoulder. She followed his gaze. Their parents loomed on the edge of the writhing knot of campers, who hugged each other and took selfies together.

Courtney's blood turned to ice. Her shaking legs took two steps back until both Riya and Colt caught her with an arm on her back.

When they were just behind her cabin mates, a small shape dashed in front of Dee. Tiny arms wrapped around Courtney's waist. She looked down to discover a tangled mass of red hair pressed against her stomach.

Courtney patted Olivia's back. The girl pulled back to stare up at her with glossy eyes.

"I'll see you next year, right?" Olivia said.

Courtney's heart twinged. "No, Liv. I'll be too old."

Olivia's freckled face pinched, her lower lip sticking out slightly. "That's not fair."

Courtney knelt, bringing her face to Olivia's level. "You have to take over for me next year, okay?"

Olivia wiped at her eyes. "How do I do that?"

Courtney placed her hands on the girl's little shoulders. "It's so easy. You just be yourself, okay? Don't let anyone tell you what to do, like we talked about."

Olivia nodded. Her green eyes shifted and stared up at Riya. She leaned forward and whispered into Courtney's ear, "Is that your girlfriend?"

Courtney hesitated, unsure how to explain. She settled on a nod.

Olivia gave her a gap-toothed grin. "She's beautiful."

Courtney smiled, tears pricking at her eyes. "Yes, she is."

"You're beautiful, too," Olivia said. "That's why you deserve each other."

Courtney laughed. It sounded so simple.

Olivia wrapped her arms around Courtney's neck, squeezing the way little kids hugged—with abandon and pure emotion.

"Goodbye, Olivia," Courtney said.

"Bye, Courtney." Olivia spotted someone else at the next table over and dashed away.

When Courtney stood, her parents stood unobstructed in

front of her. Her mother clutched a makeup-stained tissue in her hand.

"Hi," Colt said, as though nothing had changed. As though Courtney was the same girl who'd left their house four weeks ago.

Courtney swallowed. "Hi."

Silence.

"What did you think of Courtney's dance?" Colt said.

Her mother wiped at her eye with the tissue. "I'm sorry, Courtney," she said.

Courtney's brow wrinkled and she narrowed her eyes.

"I didn't realize. I didn't know. I…" She trailed off.

Courtney's dad shifted his shoulders. "What your mother is trying to say is: that dance was one of the most beautiful things I've ever seen."

Courtney pressed her lips together, trying to hold back the sobs threatening to escape.

"I didn't know how extraordinary you'd become," her mother said.

Courtney raised a fist to her lips, sniffling. Her mother reached out with two manicured hands and cradled her head. She wiped at Courtney's melting mascara with her thumbs.

Beside her, Riya smiled, breathing a sigh of relief.

"Oh," Courtney said, pulling Riya forward. Her heart pounded painfully against her ribs, but it was too late to turn back now. They'd seen the kiss. Courtney was all in. "This is Riya."

Courtney's mother looked Riya up and down without moving her head. "I remember her. From when you were children."

Courtney waited for more. But that was it. Her mother's cold appraisal and her father's silence. Their reactions weren't glowing, but still far better than Courtney expected. No yelling or ultimatums or threats, at least.

Riya's chest expanded as she pulled in a deep breath. "Good to see you again, Mr. and Mrs. Chastain," she said.

"Riya," Courtney's dad said by way of greeting. "Are your parents here?"

Oh, shit. No, that could not happen. Courtney might die from the mortification of her parents and Riya's parents having a *discussion*. That's what her dad called it when he wanted to set someone straight. She would literally die. Like, until she was dead.

"They should be arriving soon," Riya said.

"We'd like to have a discussion with them," Courtney's dad said.

"That's really not necessary," Courtney said.

Riya gave Courtney's hand a surreptitious squeeze. "It's fine, Court."

Courtney stared at Riya, trying to convey how much of a bad idea that was, but Riya either didn't notice or didn't care.

Colt clapped his hands. "It's too nice today to be wasting it in here. Let's go outside."

Her parents followed him to the door, her mom grumbling something about her heels in the soft soil.

"I have to change my shoes," Courtney called. "I'll catch up."

Steadfast, Riya stood next to Courtney.

Courtney's mother paused, frowning back at the two girls.

"Come on, Mom," Colt's voice called in to her. "There's something I want to show you."

With one final warning glance at Riya, Mrs. Chastain stepped out into the sunlight. Courtney let out a long breath.

Riya rubbed her back. "That could've gone worse."

Courtney loosed a mirthless laugh. "Just wait. They haven't talked to your parents yet."

A grin slid across Riya's full lips. It baffled Courtney.

"Why do you look so happy?"

"Courtney, my parents have raised a happily, openly bisexual daughter across four red states. They are allies. With a capital A. They're advocates. And they're not scared of your parents." The *like you are* went unspoken, mainly because Riya was too kind to say it out loud. But they both knew it was there.

Courtney sat down on the bench to untie the ribbons of her ballet slippers. "My parents—"

"Have finally met their match."

Courtney wrapped the ribbons around her slippers and retrieved her sandals from underneath a table. A flicker of hope warmed her limbs.

A couple feet before they reached the door, Riya stopped her with a hand on her arm. Courtney turned to face her. Riya slid her hands behind Courtney's neck and pulled her head down for a slow, sweet kiss.

When the two strolled outside, Courtney spotted her parents and Colt talking to a tall brown-haired white man and a stunning, petite Indian woman near the parking lot. Riya's parents.

Mr. and Mrs. Chastain's backs were to the cafeteria, but Colt stood sideways like a referee between two opposing teams. He noticed Riya and Courtney before the others and reached behind his back with his injured hand to make a subtle gesture. He pointed toward their cabin on the other side of the lake.

Courtney grabbed Riya's wrist and dashed for the spare concealment of a young tree. When they reached the full cover of the first girls' cabin, both of them burst into a fit of giggles.

Chapter Seventeen

Riya gripped Courtney's hips, pulling her closer. Closer. She didn't feel like they would ever be close enough. Courtney's soft pink lips teased Riya's mercilessly.

Everyone else had packed up and was on their way home, so they had the cabin to themselves for at least a little while longer.

Courtney swept Riya's hair into a ponytail and curled it around her wrist absent-mindedly. She gave the strands a soft tug, and they both collapsed onto Courtney's bed. Though she'd already stuffed her sheets into a bag, the bed still smelled like rose petals.

Riya traced a hand from Courtney's hip up her side, stroking the smooth bare skin between her shoulder and the tank straps of the dance leotard. Courtney loosed a soft moan that made Riya's skin sizzle.

Someone knocked on the door, and Courtney sprang off the bed, leaping to her feet. Riya tried to reason with the jolt of disappointment that shot through her. Old habits died hard, she knew. She needed to give Courtney the one thing that felt impossible: time to adjust.

Colt swung the door open three seconds after knocking. He held his good hand over his eyes. "I'm not interrupting anything, am I?"

In one smooth motion, Courtney swept her ballet shoes out of a tote bag on the floor and threw them at him. The soles slapped against his hand and flopped to the ground. Riya got the feeling it wasn't the first time she'd done exactly that.

"Ha. Ha," Courtney said.

Colt dropped his hands, smiling. He pulled keys from his pocket and tossed them to Riya. They smacked painfully against her pinkie and clattered to the floor.

Colt gave her a quizzical look. "If that were a spike, you would've bumped it perfectly."

"She can't catch," Courtney said. "Like, at all."

Riya knew she should be embarrassed by Courtney's statement, but it actually pleased her that Courtney had noticed. She'd been paying attention.

Riya scooped the keys up from the floor. She recognized the Duke University keychain immediately. "These are my dad's."

Colt just nodded, grinning.

"Why did you throw me my dad's keys?"

"Fozzie Bear basically kicked our parents out. They wanted more time to discuss 'the situation'"—he put air quotes around the phrase—"so your parents are going to ride in the car with my parents to Charlotte. And you're going to drive the three of us in your parents' car."

More time? Was that a good or bad sign? "How's it going?" Riya was almost too scared to ask.

Colt laughed. Well, that was certainly a good sign. "Your parents should've been lawyers, Riya."

Courtney burst forward. "What does that mean?"

"They're totally subversive. By the time they make

a point, my parents think they've won, but their minds are changed. It's crazy. The Johnsons have facts and numbers and even Bible verses to back up everything they say. It's like watching the twins play volleyball together." He picked up Courtney's bags with his left hand and tugged them on to his shoulder. "Let's go."

Riya picked up her own bags and followed Courtney out the door. Before Courtney closed it, Riya turned and said a silent good-bye to the place that had been her home for the past four weeks.

The place that had given Courtney Chastain back to her.

They tossed all of their bags into the trunk, and Courtney slid into the front passenger seat next to Riya. Colt stretched out on the back seat as much as he could. Once they were on the road, Colt pulled a pill bottle out of his pocket and swallowed one dry.

He met Riya's eyes in the rearview mirror, winked, and shut his eyes. Riya was lucky to have a friend like him. Courtney was downright blessed to have him as a brother. Since getting hurt, he'd done nothing but arrange miracles for Courtney. He'd probably delayed taking those painkillers, suffering who knew how much pain, so he could be sharp enough to modify and play the song.

Riya guided the car over the turns and inclines that came with driving through the mountains. She went slower than the posted speed limits partly because she wasn't comfortable with that kind of driving and partly because she was in no particular rush to get back.

Riya followed the signs for the highway until they re-entered a cell service area. Courtney switched on the GPS navigation app on her phone and announced they had two and a half hours until they reached Charlotte.

Two and a half hours until they returned to the real world.

Courtney stretched her left arm over and rested her wrist

on the seat behind Riya's head. Watching the scenery pass outside the car window, Courtney twisted her fingers into the hair at the base of Riya's neck. Flares of pleasure streaked down Riya's spine.

Riya let her foot off of the gas pedal a little bit more.

Epilogue

The final bell of the day rang out over Courtney's AP History class. She vaulted to her feet and was out the door before the rest of her classmates had managed to stand. Courtney wove easily among the rising tide of students flooding the hall toward the Anatomy classroom. Riya appeared in the doorway, head turned sideways, chatting excitedly with one of her teammates about that night's game. It was the first one of the season, and Riya had been worrying about it constantly.

It was two weeks into the school year, so she'd seen Riya in her school uniform at least ten times. Still, every time, it stopped Courtney in her tracks. She'd always thought the uniforms were dumb and unflattering to everyone, but Riya had proven her totally wrong. She was a vision in the plaid skirt, navy tights, and matching navy blazer. Seriously, it was unfair to every other girl there.

The Johnsons had somehow negotiated a tense peace between her and her parents. The Chastains were not happy about this "phase"—their word—but they didn't openly hinder her relationship with Riya. "At least you can't get pregnant with a girl," her dad had said. Out loud. In front of Riya. Courtney had blushed so hard she thought blood might rush out of her eyeballs.

And, bonus, they stopped trying to set her up with "nice young men," aka the spawn of their political allies and work acquaintances.

They were more supportive of her dancing, though, promising to attend a couple of her upcoming performances. They hadn't been to a recital since she was eleven, so she wasn't holding her breath, but there was hope. Her mom had begrudgingly admitted that Courtney would still be able to attend law school even if she studied dance during undergrad. It was a start.

The students at St John's had been hit or miss. A few were openly hostile—Bridget hadn't been the last person she'd heard use the d-word—but most of them didn't even seem to notice. She was sure plenty of people gossiped behind her back, but, somehow, Courtney couldn't get herself worked up over it. She had Colt, Riya, and her closest friends. She didn't need much else. If other people wanted to waste their time gossiping about her, she felt sorry for them.

The moment Riya saw her in the hallway, her face lit up. Courtney smiled. She slipped an arm over Riya's shoulders and kissed the top of her head.

"You coming to the game tonight?" Riya asked.

Courtney stopped suddenly, fighting a smirk. "That's tonight? Crap, I have to do this thing."

Riya's smile slipped until Courtney burst out laughing. She tugged open the two buttons on her blazer, then pulled the sides wide open.

She'd spent an hour last night painting on her shirt with glittery puff paint. It read "You Got Served" on top with a volleyball below, "#4" scrawled across the ball. She hadn't planned on showing it to Riya until the game, but she'd been dying to reveal it all day and couldn't wait any longer.

She'd made one for Colt, too. He'd complain, but he'd wear it.

"Nice," Riya's teammate said, admiring the shirt. "You know the lines on the volleyball are wrong, though, right?"

Courtney dropped her head, staring at the ball with narrowed eyes. She frowned. "Are they?"

Riya placed a hand on each side of Courtney's face and lifted her head up.

"Nope, it's perfect." A grin stretched fully across Riya's face. "Courtney Chastain, I think I'm going to keep you."

Courtney returned her smile. "Riya Johnson, I'm not going to give you a choice."

Acknowledgments

First, I must send a thousand kisses to Mohammed, without whom I literally wouldn't have survived writing this book. Thank you for cooking my meals and taking care of everything while I wrote, and for keeping me from a panic attack when I thought I'd lost all my edits. I love you to Andromeda and back.

My undying appreciation goes to my agent, Rebecca Podos, for everything, but especially for supporting me veering off plan a bit so I could write this book. I can't thank Stacy Abrams enough for shaping this story and pushing me to make it better at each step. Everyone on my Entangled team—Liz, Alycia, Christine, Heather, Debbie, Melanie, Katie, Beth, and more I haven't yet "met"—y'all are the best in the business and I'm so thrilled to be part of the family.

I know I kind of disappeared from the world while I wrote this book, so I have to give a shout-out to my friends and wally players who welcomed me back with only a little good-natured grumbling. I'll always come back for y'all.

About the Author

Sarah is a 30-something YA author who currently lives in Orlando with a 60-lb mutt who thinks he's a Chihuahua. She believes that some boys are worth trusting, all girls have power, and dragons are people, too.

She's a proud member of the Gator Nation and has a BS in Mechanical Engineering, but has switched careers entirely. She now works as an Event Planner for a County Library.

Find out more about her at www.sarahnicolas.com, and check her out on twitter @sarah_nicolas.

Discover more of Entangled Teen Crush's books...

DEFYING GRAVITY
a *Finding Perfect* novel by Kendra C. Highley

Zoey Miller lives for her holidays in Aspen. Her time up on the mountain with the Madison brothers, Parker and Luke, is everything. But for the first time, it's not enough. Now she's determined to win one of the brothers' hearts. The brother she has in mind is a renowned player, with hordes of snow-bunnies following him around Snowmass resort. And the other...well, he's her best friend and knows she deserves better. Namely him. And *he's* going to win *her* heart.

THE BOYFRIEND BET
a *Boyfriend Chronicles* novel by Chris Cannon

Zoe Cain knows that Grant Evertide, her brother's number-one nemesis, is way out of her league. So naturally, she kisses him. She's thrilled when they start dating, non-exclusively, but Zoe's brother claims Grant is trying to make her his "Ringer," an oh-so-charming tradition where a popular guy dates a non-popular girl until he hooks up with her, then dumps her. Zoe threatens to neuter Grant with hedge clippers if he's lying, but Grant swears he isn't trying to trick her. Still, that doesn't mean Grant is the commitment type—even if winning a bet is on the line.

Discover the **Endless Summer** *series*

DARING THE BAD BOY

Also by Sarah Nicolas...

DRAGONS ARE PEOPLE, TOO

CPSIA information can be obtained
at www.ICGtesting.com
Printed in the USA
LVOW12s1540160917
548593LV00001B/5/P